The Malediction of Oak Grove

THE MALEDICTION OF OAK GROVE

JENNIFER ZAMBONI

Paperback ISBN 978-1-7372911-3-8

kdp ASIN B0CH92BNT6

Draft2digital ISBN 9798223103448

Cover created by Burning Phoenix Covers:
www.burningphoenixcovers.com

Edited by LeaVPA

 Created with Vellum

For the Nomadic Guild of Scripturants:
We may be be a bit scattered these days, but I couldn't have done any
of this without you.

I

Secrets and whispers spread from sapling to elder oak through newly budded spring leaves riffling in the breeze.

Middle-aged men, boots crunching around the underbrush and over the decaying leaves, passed through their midst.

The occasional hikers tromped through, but these were different. Their boots were too new, their clothing better suited for offices than making their way through the grabbing thorns of the raspberry brambles that appeared dead to the untrained eye.

A man with balding gray hair slapped a sturdy tree with an open palm and started a discussion about money and acreage while another, flipping over the top sheet of paper on a yellow legal pad, jotted notes with the expensive silver ballpoint pen his boss handed him moments before. Discussion moved from business to the trees themselves.

"So, we have several logging companies ready to start bidding for the job, yes?" the first man asked, dusting his hands off on his navy slacks leaving little bits of aged bark on his thighs.

"We do." The man with the notepad flipped back to the previous page, then turned it so the others could see the list of prospective companies.

"Excellent. Next town meeting we'll put it to vote. I have your guarantee, don't I boys?" The balding man spread his arms wide to indicate the little group, who hung on to his every word.

He was answered with a chorus of "You betcha, boss" and "Of course."

"Wonderful, wonderful. We've got this in the bag. In a few short months, these beauties will all be headed to the saw mill. Woods filled with this much healthy oak are pretty much unheard of. We should make a nice paycheck off it."

"Hope the dryad doesn't get angry when her grove is clear cut," another man guffawed.

"She is important to our image. Old legends are good like that. And we'll keep her sexy statue and a few trees for the tourists to visit. More money in the bank."

Echoes of clear cut carried on the breeze.

Clear cut.

Clear cut. Clear cut. Clear cut. Clear-cut. Clear-cut!

It jangled through the leaves until reaching a massive oak at the center of the wood. The echoes sank through the roots, bark, and sap awakening the being deep within at long last.

CLEAR CUT!

The dryad was pulled to awareness, feeling the tree and its essence surrounding her, feeling its distress. The deep wrongness slipped into her, festering her out of the tree like an infection. Out and out and out until she blinked in the bright afternoon sun of April 16th.

Shivering, she created a glamour of clothing over her lithe, nude form: a long green dress drifting in waving gossamer from her hips and a circlet of twigs and acorns tangling in her hair.

She gazed up at the sky with dark eyes rimmed with even darker lashes. The birds were still. The insects, just coming out to play, told her nothing. The wind blew, gusting through the leaves whispering *Clear cut!* once more.

Clear cutting? Here? She had a pact with the residents of Oak Grove. They would never cut her trees, and in return they could live in peace and prosperity at her borders.

She touched a long-fingered hand to the bark of another tree, listening to everything it had to say. It hadn't been there when she'd gone to sleep. In fact, her grove was more densely populated than she'd left it, which pleased her to no end. Through her connection, she felt the growth of the forest and the centuries that had passed since she'd gone to sleep. Even the tree she'd just emerged from was a descendent of the original.

Who wanted to destroy her home?

A chickadee alighted on her shoulder, fluttering its black and white wings and fluffing its feathers so that it resembled an off-color tennis ball.

"Hello, little friend," she whispered, her voice useless for the time being. "Who is it that seeks to destroy our home?"

The chickadee took to the air, and Feya raced after it, dodging around trees, leaping over ancient roots, until it settled on a branch. She froze as the thump and crunch of footsteps filled the air.

She sank into the bark of a tree in order to watch and listen undetected.

"I think this one in particular would make a good-sized coffee table. What do you fellas think? We could have them sold as souvenirs and family heirlooms. A piece of the Grove to pass down to future generations along with the tall-tale."

"Tie a flag around it, and we'll make a note of it, eh Jerry?" The balding man slapped the man holding the paper on the back.

"You bet your butt." He pulled a roll of flagging tape out of his jacket pocket and handed it to the man admiring the tree Feya was currently sharing space with.

Tearing a generous length of fluorescent orange plastic, he looped it around and tied a tight knot.

They traipsed back down the path they'd come by, leaving Feya and the chickadee in their wake.

Pushing out of the tree, Feya smoothed her dress.

This wouldn't do at all. These men were different than those from her last visit to the human world. Their clothes sounded odd, as if they were no longer made from plants or animals. Their scents acrid and false.

She looked down at her green gown and frowned. Before she approached any humans, she would find out what she needed to blend in. But first, she needed to check on her trees, wanting to greet all the new saplings, and pay her respects to those that had fallen over the years and became a part of the soil that the younger ones grew in.

"Keep me informed of who enters these woods, little friend," Feya said then waved as the little black and white creature took to the air once more.

It would take time to become fully reacquainted with her territory as she worked in a spiral that slowly moved her from her home tree towards the edge of the woods.

Squirrels, chipmunks, and rabbits left signs everywhere. Openings at the roots of trees which were turned into burrows and piles of acorns that had been forgotten in the depth of winter. Scat and tracks littered the area. Birds gathered everywhere: chickadees, blue jays, crows, a screech owl, a couple kestrels, and a band of turkey vultures. She would need to befriend them all if she wanted their cooperation.

She loved her oaks, old and young, all descended from her tree of origin. The undergrowth thrived as well—raspberry brambles, ferns, and even a small gathering of lady slippers, which never grew this far north. They didn't fall under her influence, but they did live in harmony with the creatures here, so she would protect them as well.

Around and around, weaving here and there, speaking encouragements to the youngest saplings as she moved with the grace of the fae. All the trees were healthy and strong, minus a few elderly matrons that had lived good lives and were slowly fading. These, she pressed her forehead to, thanking them for their work and helping them to move on in peace. When they finally ceased, she would help ease their bodies into the ground in order to nourish their descendants.

She happened upon boot tracks, most likely belonging to the men she'd witnessed earlier, and she followed their path.

The trees thinned towards the edge of town, which stretched farther than she ever imagined possible. These younger, slimmer trees had more space to spread their branches, to soak up the sun and rain. As she approached, voices she'd heard not so long-ago rode the breeze to her ears as they approached the outskirts of the grove.

There, they halted by a statue carved from a tree that had fallen a century ago. According to the plaque at its base, the statue was meant to be the likeness of the Oak Grove Dryad.

Feya edged around to get a better look. The woman featured there was nude, her arms, legs and hair sunk deep into the tree she emerged from. Bare breasts thrust towards the sky. A wreath of oak leaves and acorns adorned her brow.

It doesn't look much like me, Feya thought. And it wasn't here before. Someone must have created it from a description. And indeed, it was. At the bottom of the plaque was stamped the artist's name and the year 1843. Years beyond when she'd walked among men. The town had been but a few families and a church, hours of travel away from the next town by horseback, secluded so they could live their lives in peace, away from the tyrannical rule of the puritans.

The man named Jerry reached up and palmed the hard breast.

"Too bad she's just a myth," he said, pretending to squeeze. "I would be down for a good fuck in the woods."

"Who wouldn't be?" the balding man asked, also approaching the statue and sliding his meaty fingers from the knee up the inside of one thigh.

The tree Feya spied from cracked and groaned, giving voice to her anger. While it wasn't an accurate portrayal of her body, it represented her, and she felt violated. If there had been a dead tree nearby, she would have dropped it on their lecherous heads.

This was why she'd stayed away from humans for all those hundreds of years before the people of Oak Grove had come to her. But those families, when she'd revealed herself to them, had befriended her. She'd helped them with gifts of the fresh remains of trees, who's sap had just ceased to flow, for fuel for their fires and for building materials. In turn, they'd shared the ashes with her, returning the nourishment. She'd protected them from outsiders, causing them to lose direction, and when at last she was assured that they would continue the work they'd started together, she'd retreated and slept.

But these men—these disgusting creatures—were talking about taking what she would never give them, bodily or from her home. These were not the descendants of those good people. These were something else, predators that she'd previously kept away. Despite all the protection she'd laid over the land, despite the feral magic that saturated it, they'd found their way in and pushed her influence out. All without her ever knowing. They'd kept true to the bargain, leaving her grove in peace, not taking what wasn't given. Now, she was a bedtime story. Something to sell to bring more strangers to her path. She seethed as they finally walked away, leaving the statue, parking lot, and picnic area in silence.

She pulled away from the tree, and approached the statue herself. While it wasn't a true likeness, it was a beautiful piece of art, a study of the female form married with nature.

Brilliant green moss crawled up one side of the carving, and she lightly ran her fingers over the velvety softness. Again, it wasn't hers, but it was an organism that lived alongside her own. She dug her toes into the dirt, sinking roots down and gathering water. She carefully peeled away a small section of moss and cupped it in her hand, mixing it with the water pulled from her roots. With a gentle finger, she set about creating a loose garment of moss to cover the statue. It wasn't the nudity that bothered her. She couldn't care less about clothes as they were merely a tool to help her fit in, but the way those men had treated this beautiful work was not alright.

Those parts would be hidden from prying eyes when she finished.

The moss grew quickly under her encouragement. As she finished, she gave the new growth just the barest stroke in thanks before leaving the tree line to scout the best route through town.

Long ago, she'd gifted each family with a young sapling to keep watch over their homes, instructing that they must never be cut and only be put to other uses once the essence of life had faded from them. The gift was not only so the trees could watch but also a way for her to travel unseen.

She would assess these people, determine if there was any goodness left in them or if these men were a true example of what the town had to offer.

Moving slowly from tree to tree, the whispers of *clear cut, clear cut* continued on the wind.

2

eya watched the town for several days, needing to determine who would be best for her first contact. She'd come to a decision, and it was time to move forward with her plan.

Main street was a busy avenue with far more buildings than she remembered, not to mention the stink of the horseless metal wagons that sped every which way. Almost all the humans wore those strange clothes, but she still hadn't dared get close enough to create an accurate imitation to replace her dress.

From tree to tree, she flitted, waiting for eyes to look away before she made each move. The church she was currently lurking in the shadow bore remnants of the original building: the stones it sat on, mostly, but also the stained-glass window an artisan had gifted the congregation long ago.

He had been a traveling man who the church had taken in during the depths of winter. He'd been in a bad way. Frost bite had claimed several of his toes and the first joint of the second finger on his left hand, and he'd been hypothermic.

They'd warmed him up and cared for him right in the sanctuary after a congregant had found him unconscious in a snow drift on his way to Sunday service. The preacher and his pregnant wife had taken him in, helping him regain his health and strength. He was there for the birth during one of the worst blizzards of the decade. His nimble fingers had been able to turn the breeched babe, allowing it to come safely into the world and his mother to survive the ordeal in a time when death in childbirth was common.

He'd remained in the area for three years, building a little cabin for himself and practicing his trade making those beautiful windows for the church and several other local buildings. When he finished, he'd thanked the town, given his gifts, installed them himself, then vanished the next day. They'd called him an angel in disguise, but Feya had known he'd been an ordinary mortal man. A good man, to be sure, but just a man.

His cabin used to reside at the very edge of her grove, and she'd spent many a day there talking about life, where he'd come from, what his plans had been before his near-death experience. What had started as a mere friendship developed into the more intimate path of lovers. She'd spent many daylight hours naked, lounging on his bed, his rough fingers exploring her sensitive skin, his mouth on her and hers on his. Every moment was an expression of mutual appreciation. When it was time for him to leave, he'd spent the night worshiping her body. Usually, she returned to her trees once the sun was spent, but she'd known it was his time, even if he hadn't said the words. They'd reveled in each other's comfort late into the night, eventually falling asleep, her wrapped tight in his strong arms.

When she woke the next morning, his side of the bed was cold, and he was gone. A little glass acorn pendant, topped with a natural cap, had been lying on his pillow. She'd worn that little charm on a length of yarn around her neck until she'd slipped deep into the bark of her tree to rest until the trees had begged her to wake up once more.

She touched the empty hollow of her throat, where the necklace once lay. It had disappeared, probably becoming part of the forest floor. She hoped to find it one day. The memories it held were ones she never wanted to forget. That man, who's name she could no longer remember, had been part of an important moment in her life. A simple moment of pure happiness.

Across the street stood a little shop, painted white, with a sign posted out front announcing fresh flowers within. Behind it stood several green houses. The natural energy that bled from the property called to her; kindred souls in leafy mantles.

Feya watched the woman there. She always had a smile for whomever she spoke with. She spent any spare time outside tending the flower gardens, only going inside when a customer approached or it was time to shut down for the day. Everything about the woman drew Feya, and she just knew this was a human she could trust.

She hadn't made the leap across the wide length of faded black asphalt yet. It felt strange under her feet when she'd stepped on it the night before. Her toes couldn't stretch down through it to feel the earth below. She'd wrinkled her nose, then washed her feet in a puddle, soaking up the moisture.

But today, she knew she had to cross, to speak with the

woman. She had decided to wait until evening, when the woman would flip the sign in the door and turn off the lights.

She rested patiently in her tree as the sun rose, arced, then descended, painting the sky a brilliant shade of pink with accents of orange. The woman glanced down at the band wrapped around her wrist and stood, brushing damp earth off her knees, and headed into the building.

Metal carriages passed, and Feya waited until she was sure no one would see her. She pushed her way out of the tree, dashed across the asphalt, up the drive, and to the front door, catching it just as the woman was reaching to lock it. The woman's eyes flew wide, and she backed away, her hands raised.

Feya entered, shutting then locking the door behind her. When she was sure they wouldn't be interrupted, Feya turned to the stunned woman.

"Hello," she said, clasping her hands behind her back, attempting to look less threatening.

"Uh, hi." The woman gave her a little wave from her safe distance. "Who are you?"

"Feya." The dryad waited to see if there was any recognition of her name, but the woman simply stood waiting patiently without any sign of understanding.

"Okay." The woman's eyebrows scrunched together and she bit one side of her lower lip.

"What's your name?" Feya asked, stepping forward, her bare feet soundless on the wooden floor.

The woman stepped back. "I'm Tabitha."

She straightened and pulled her shoulders back, regaining her composure over the unusual moment she was having. "How can I help you, Feya?"

"I do need your help." Feya stepped forward again.

This time, Tabitha stood her ground. "So I gathered,

but what is it you're looking for?" She looked Feya up and down, blinking. "Is there a Renaissance Fest going on? Are you lost?"

"No, I'm not lost. This is my home."

The human woman studied her face, frowning. "Is it? I don't think we've ever met."

Feya nodded. "We haven't."

"Where do you live?"

"In the grove," said Feya matter-of-factly, pointing one thumb over her shoulder in the general direction.

"The grove…" Tabitha's eyes bore all the confusion she must have been feeling.

"Yes. The grove has been my home for hundreds of years."

The woman's eyebrows knit together. "Hundreds of years. Who did you say you were again?"

"Feya. I'm your dryad." Her face broke into a wide smile as she bounced lightly on her toes a couple times.

Tabitha spluttered, "Excuse me, what now?"

"You know, that statue right outside the grove, with the plaque? That's me. Well, not me exactly, but a depiction of me. I was here long before the founding of this town. When you humans arrived, we lived well together, but I eventually tired and fell into the deep sleep."

Tabitha backed to the counter, resting her weight there. *Was this woman delusional?* She wondered.

"Here, I'll show you." Feya grabbed Tabitha's arm and hauled her out the back door and out to the grand oak growing several yards away from the building. She stood Tabitha to one side, who complied in stunned silence.

"Stay there and watch." Feya rested her palm on the bark, allowing the tree to soak her in.

Tabitha ran forward with a small shriek, then jumped back again as Feya reemerged.

"See? I'm the dryad." She patted the tree in thanks.

"I've lost it," Tabitha muttered. "It's finally happening."

"No, I think you're fine. I've been watching you for a few days now, and you seem like a perfectly rational human."

"You—I—you…"

"Let's go back inside and talk, okay?" Feya took Tabitha's arm again, and led her back into the shop, helping the woman onto a stool.

She opened the door to the back room and explored until she found a cup and figured out the odd water pump.

She was delighted when her senses drew her to the metal contraption with a pipe and knobs in the counter. Water gushed out, and Feya laughed, splashing her fingers through it. "This is amazing! Of all the things I missed, I think this one is actually a good one!" She filled a clear cup, hurried back, and thrust it into Tabitha's fingers. She ran back then took another and filled it to the brim, drinking it down, then filling it again, drinking it, then set the cup on the counter.

"Absolutely marvelous!" she exclaimed, turning back to Tabitha, who was gaping at her.

"Are you sure I haven't lost it?" Tabitha asked, spilling her overfilled glass a bit as she brought it to her lips. Maybe she was dehydrated and was hallucinating. She knew very well that she'd filled her water bottle several times that day, but her mind needed an explanation for what was going on in front of her.

"You're fine." Feya waved a hand. "But like I said, I've been watching, and I think I can trust you. Can I trust you, Tabitha?"

"Call me Tabby," the woman replied automatically. "I mean, sure. I think you can trust me."

"Alright then, like I said. I'm the dryad, and I've been asleep for a very long time. Obviously, things have changed since I last took a walk." She picked at her deep green gown, then smoothed it. "Have humans entirely stopped clothing themselves in natural materials?"

Tabby tilted her head in thought. "A lot have, yes. Plastic is cheaper, and that's the basis for a lot of fabrics, I think. But there's still wool and cotton around."

Feya rolled her lips between her teeth then asked, "Plastic?"

"Yeah, a lot is made out of it. It's—It's… I think plastic is made from fossil fuels or something. I can find out for you, if you'd like."

"Yes please." She nodded eagerly. "How long will it take for you to hear back? How do letters travel these days?"

"What?"

"How do you make your correspondences?"

"The U.S. Postal service. A truck comes and picks up the mail and drops off the new stuff."

"A truck?" Feya racked her brain for the word and came up with nothing.

"Oh boy, we do have a lot to go over, don't we?"

This time it was Tabby who took Feya's arm and ushered her out the door.

SEVERAL HOURS LATER, Tabby had Feya sitting in her kitchen, dressed in a pair of jeans and a soft cotton tee shirt. Several print outs and books were spread over the table for the women to study.

The dryad was so deeply engrossed in the text that she didn't even notice when the door opened, and a lanky teenage boy walked in, stopping dead at the sight of her.

"Mom? Who's your friend?" he asked, openly gawking.

"This is Feya." Tabby bustled around the kitchen, heating a plate of dinner for her son, who had been working at the local coffee shop all evening. "She's going to be around for a while."

Feya's head popped up at the sound of her name. "What?"

"Feya, this is my son, Lucas." She slung her arm around him, just below his shoulders, giving him an affectionate squeeze.

"You can call me Luke," the boy said, holding out a hand in greeting.

Feya shook it. "A pleasure to meet you, Lucas—I mean Luke." She turned her attention back to the books in front of her.

The boy raised his eyebrows in question at his mother as she set his plate on the counter for him. "Later," she mouthed, kissing her boy's cheek.

He nodded. "No Tim tonight?"

Tabby shook her head. "He won't be by until late." She nodded her head in Feya's direction again.

Feya closed the book and stretched. "I think that's enough learning for one day. Mind if I have another glass of water before I find a tree?"

"Not at all." Tabby filled a tall glass and watched the dryad guzzle it down in seconds.

"Thanks. Good night, Tabby, Luke. Would you mind if I continued reading tomorrow?"

"Not at all. I'll show you how to use the computer, and you'll have all the knowledge of the world at your fingertips."

Feya gave her a quizzical look. "All right, thanks. See you in the morning then. I'll see myself out."

She strode to the back door, and walked off the back porch.

"Watch," Tabby whispered, tugging her son to the window.

They both kept their eyes glued to the oak in the back yard as Feya sank into it without a trace.

Luke's jaw dropped. "Whoa." He looked to his mother for confirmation that he saw what he thought he did.

Tabby nodded slowly. "Yeah."

3

Tabby turned from the window to gauge her son's reaction.

"What the actual fuck?" Luke's eyes remained glued to the tree, almost as if he was afraid to blink and miss something.

"Language, young man," Tabby teased, bumping his shoulder with her own. "No, really, I agree. She showed up at the shop while I was closing today."

She filled her son in on all the details she could remember of her initial encounter, then hopped up on a bar stool and took a sip of her water.

"Whoa." He collapsed on the stool next to hers. "Um, so, what do we do?"

"Beats me. It's kind of news to me that dryads are real and not just something out of C.S. Lewis's imagination. What's next, talking beavers?"

"I hope not," Luke grimaced in mock horror, his shoulders shuddering.

Tabby thumped his arm, following his line of thought. "Not like that, you little pervert!"

"What? I'm a healthy teenage boy. Of course my mind goes straight to lady beaver—"

She covered her ears with her palms. "La-la-la, I can't hear you!"

"Isn't it your job as my parent to educate me about sex?" he hollered over her, dodging another swat from his mother.

"You've apparently gone and gotten an education without me. And if I ever hear you call a vagina a beaver again, I'm going to tell the world that you wouldn't let the tooth fairy take your first tooth because you were convinced she'd use it to put a spell on you."

"Ew, Mom! You said vagina." Scrunching his face, he faked a gag and leaned back as if to get as far away from the word as he could without actually moving.

"Yes. Yes I did. And did you know I have one… and that I squashed your big head out of it?" She waggled her head with each word then mimed, with hands apart as if gripping a melon, pulling a baby head away from her abdomen.

"Moooom!" Luke banged his forehead on the counter with thump.

She patted the back of his head. "There, there, dear."

He tilted his head to rest on his chin. "How did you get the upper hand in this conversation?"

She clasped her hands and leaned closer. "Years and years of practice, young padawan."

"You're so weird." He shifted again to sit up while rolling his eyes.

"And you take after me." She batted her eyelashes.

"Whatever. So what are we going to do with the mythological creature currently sleeping in our backyard?" He jerked his thumb at the window.

Tabby tapped her chin, debating. She hadn't had much

of an opportunity to come up with a plan for the issue that had hurled itself into her lap. "First, you're going to teach her how to use the internet. In the meantime, I guess I'm going to do some research on the Oak Grove Dryad." She'd heard the story growing up, but couldn't recall it in any detail.

"Maybe we can charge tourists to see her disappear into trees!" Luke pointed a finger in the air. "We'll be rich, and then we'll own this town."

She shook her head before he even finished his sentence. She suspected he was joking but still. "I don't think I agree with that plan. Plus, something tells me Feya wouldn't be so cool with that. Want to go to the historical society with me, after you get her set up on the computer tomorrow?"

Luke shrugged his shoulders. "Sure, I guess so. Mind if I take the rest of this up to my room? I've got a ton of homework." He tapped his fork on his half full plate.

"Of course. Just don't forget to bring your dirty dishes to the sink before you go to bed."

"Sure, Mom." Luke gathered his discarded backpack then his meal and headed up to his room.

Tabby wandered into the living room to boot up the family computer.

Her cat, Peaky, jumped onto her lap and curled up in a giant purring loaf. Computer time was his favorite time.

Absent-mindedly, she stroked his fluff while she entered dryad into the search bar. Article after article popped up, mostly pertaining to Greek mythology and a little bit of Celtic lore, but nothing about Dryads in the United States.

Her search did reveal that dryad were traditionally the spirit of oak trees, sometimes beginning their lives as human before becoming cursed or gifted by the gods.

She tried for local folklore, and all she got was bits

about little mischievous people reported by the natives in the area over the years. But they tended to wreak havoc, not become some type of land protectors. She sighed and rubbed her eyes. It had been a long day.

"Come on, Peaky, let's get you some chow."

He trilled as she stood, then trotted ahead of her to lead the way to his food bowl.

As the sun breached the horizon, a knock on the back door woke Tabby from a particularly good dream featuring a shirtless Chris Hemsworth.

"Damn," she muttered, squinting at her cell phone. She had a pretty good guess who was messing with her beauty sleep, but that didn't mean she wanted to go do something about it.

The knock sounded again, more insistent in rhythm and volume.

Tabby muttered under her breath as she toed on a pair of ratty old slippers and pulled a sweatshirt over her tank top. People who woke others at the ass crack of dawn didn't get greeted with bras on.

Feya stood on the back step, looking as fresh as a daisy.

Tabby opened the door and motioned her in, eyelids drooping as she muffled a yawn in the bend of her elbow.

"Can I get you anything? Coffee? Water? Cereal?"

"I'd love a glass of water, thank you," said Feya, making herself at home at the table, and busying herself with the books.

Tabby filled a glass and set it before her. "Luke will get you set up on the computer after he wakes up. We won't poke the bear until then."

"Your son is a werebear or a skinwalker?" Feya asked, eyebrows raised.

"What? No! It's just a figure of speech. It means he

gets super cranky if he gets woken up. Are those things real?"

"Weres and skinwalkers?" Feya nodded emphatically. "Of course. At least they were. I haven't come across any in your books, so maybe they died out."

Tabby nodded slowly. "Huh, well you learn something new every day, I guess."

"I try to," said Feya.

"Oh. Good." Tabby shuffled over to her Keurig, popped in a pod, and stuck a mug under the spout to catch the glorious magic bean water it produced.

As it emitted a loud sputtering spurt, Feya spun around in alarm.

"What is that horrid sound?" Her eyes were wide with alarm.

"Just my coffee." Tabby lifted her mug after the final hiss and set it on the counter to cool for a moment.

"I've never had coffee. I don't think it was here last time I was awake."

"Maybe that's why you slept so long," Tabby muttered, gathering eggs, sausage, peppers, and cheese to start making breakfast.

She got a pan sizzling hot and began scrambling everything together before starting toast.

A slow thumping came from the stairs. Moments later, Luke stumbled into the kitchen wearing only a pair of black cotton shorts. "Coooffeeee," he moaned.

Without even looking, Tabby pressed a button and started the Keurig all over again. She'd known her kid would be down the stairs as soon as the smell of breakfast cooking wafted under his door, so she had everything set up.

He wobbled forward and grabbed the mug, sipping gingerly. "Hoooot."

"Well yes, that is what the machine does. Why don't you have a seat before you tip over." Tabby nudged him towards a stool.

Feya watched without a word, soaking it all in.

The toaster dinged, and Luke stood to help his mom then dug into the meal with the vigor of a starving man.

"How are you still growing," Tabby muttered, plopping extra eggs onto his plate after he cleared half of it between one breath and the next.

He shrugged his broadening shoulders and continued chewing.

"He's a very well-built young man. Muscles like that need a lot of fuel," Feya pointed out.

"You betcha." Luke flexed his arms, making his biceps pop.

"Hey, kiddo, why don't you go put on a shirt, m'kay?" Tabby patted his head.

"Really, Mom?" He pulled his head away from her touch.

"Go." She pointed at the stairs.

Luke shoved in one more giant mouthful then dashed up to his room.

"It was just an observation." Feya's eyebrows knit in confusion as her gaze turned back to Tabby.

"And he's just a child." Tabby busied herself cleaning up and making her own plate.

Feya's head cocked to the side. "In my day, he could marry and father children."

Tabby scowled. "Yeah well, this is my day and my house. He gets to be a kid for a little while longer."

"I'm sorry, I didn't mean to offend." Feya wrung her hands together, biting her lip.

Tabby waved her off. "Don't worry about it." This odd

creature was all at once ancient and naïve with a current of unspeakable power.

Luke reemerged wearing a sleeveless tee. "Better?" he asked, plucking at the thin fabric.

"Much," said Tabby.

"Good. These guns need some suns." He rotated one arm, inspecting for tan lines.

Her smile was warm as she gave him a single finger gun and a wink. "You do you, boo."

"Except go shirtless."

"Exactly. Now, finish getting ready for the day so you can show Feya how to use the computer."

Getting Feya competent with the computer took much longer than anticipated.

Tabby checked the time yet again. "You know, I think I'm going to check in at the shop. Meet me there when you're finished, okay Lucas?"

He raised his eyebrows. "Why mother, are you saying you trust me alone with this stunning creature?"

Feya preened under the praise, but kept her eyes glued to what she was doing.

Tabby shook her finger at the teenage boy. "Behave, you two!"

She grabbed her coat and her keys then escaped.

Feya had been charming and personable so far, but Tabby simply didn't have the patience after being woken up before she was ready. Perhaps she was a bear too.

The short drive to the shop soothed her, helped along by the hot coffee in her favorite teal travel mug. She pulled into her usual spot alongside the building, unbuckled, then headed around back to the green houses.

Sara, a young woman that had been working at the shop for several years now, had already opened for the day and was half way through watering the plants.

"How is everything this morning?" Tabby asked, taking notes on the plants in a pocket-sized notebook. There were a few that needed cutting back in order to become fuller, more pleasing to the eye when they eventually made it out to the sales tent.

"Good. Almost done watering. Everyone looks healthy and happy." Sara dusted her dirt covered hands on her overalls.

"Perfect. I'll get out of your hair in just a sec. Is there anything you need while I'm right here?"

"Actually, yeah. I left my water in the car, would you mind manning the hose while I go grab it?"

"Of course," said Tabby, accepting the nozzle.

Pointing it at the next row of pots, she put gentle pressure on the trigger releasing a dense mist to soak into the soil. The scent of damp earth filled the air, and she sighed in contentment.

"Thank you so much!" Sara reclaimed the hose, then unscrewed the cap of her water and took a couple big gulps.

"Any time. I'll just be puttering until my son gets here. Errands today!"

"Well, have fun. I think I'm good here!" She continued watering the plants all the way down the row with patient progress, taking care that each pot got what it needed.

"THAT WAS AN EXPERIENCE," said Luke.

Tabby linked arms with him as they walked down the road together. "How'd it go after I left?"

"Uh, all right I guess, for giving someone a crash course in the development of technology over the past hundred years or so. At least she can read and catches on quick, that's all I can say."

She gave his arm a reassuring squeeze. "I'm sorry, kiddo."

"Eh, it's all right. She's nice enough. Very open with the compliments." He looked down at her and waggled his eyebrows.

"Ya don't say there, muscle man." She poked her son's bicep.

"Well, at least someone appreciates all the hard work I put in."

"I'd appreciate it more if I didn't keep having to buying you new clothes since you decided to turn into the Hulk."

Luke guffawed. "Well, at least I'm pretty… just like my mama."

"You're a suck up, and I love you." She leaned her head against his shoulder.

He kissed the top of her head then said, "Love you too, Mom."

The historical society resided in a large house that belonged to a former mayor and had been maintained with pristine standards. The brick building was preceded by white pillars which framed the double doors, holding up an extended roof.

A bell tinkled above the door as they entered. Inside appeared dim after walking around in the bright sun.

A couple little old ladies waved from a fainting couch where they sat crocheting and gossiping. The building was filled with historical town artifacts and was run by volunteers who all seemed to be over the age of 70, loved ostentatious hats, and always had a pot of tea ready.

"Tabby, Lucas, is there anything I can do for you today?" One set aside her project and stood to greet them, smoothing her long skirt then adjusting the high neck of her blouse which was secured by an antique silhouette broach. Her short curly white hair was mostly covered by a magenta straw hat, bedecked with dried wild flowers.

"Hi, Betty!" said Tabby, a smile spreading over her features. Betty had been a constant in her life, having taught several generations of third graders before her retirement.

"Betty, still the loveliest girl in town, I see." Lucas bounded over and kissed her cheek.

"Hey, what about me?" the other lady asked, also rising and wearing an equally large straw hat in sky blue.

"Why Clara, I thought I was seeing double. So much beauty going on over here!"

Clara turned her cheek to receive Luke's kiss.

"Shameless flirt," she giggled, patting his cheek with one lace-gloved hand.

Tabby just shook her head. "I could use some help, actually. I need to know everything you know about the Oak Grove Dryad."

"Oh, I'm sure you already know everything there is. The stories are more to entertain tourists and children," said Betty.

"Well, entertain me anyhow. Something came up, and I want to make sure I've got my story straight."

"Fine, fine, come on then, you two." Betty motioned for them to follow.

Betty and Clara linked arms with one another and led them down the hall to the display.

"Here we are, everything we have on the dryad," said Clara, gesturing at the art covering the walls from floor to ceiling; everything from professional paintings to children's stick figure crayon drawings.

"Would you like me to tell you the story my grandmother told me and my brothers?" Betty asked.

"Absolutely," said Tabby, wandering around to study each illustration.

Betty took a seat in the rocking chair and clasped her hands in her lap.

"Long, long ago," she began, her eyes studying a drawing on the opposite wall through thick lensed cat eye glasses. "Before there were any towns in this area, there stood an enormous oak. A big, beautiful specimen with a glorious canopy and a colossal trunk."

Her crackling voice took on a whimsical air as she continued her tale. "Our ancestors found a beautiful old oak tree when they fled the persecution of their puritan neighbors. It was secluded and far, far away from their colony where no one would find them for years to come.

"Something about the tree told them that this was home, and they began building houses nearby.

"A young man began cutting down a sapling when a woman appeared, bare except for her long green hair, and fell to her knees before him, begging him not to harm her trees.

"He removed his coat, and flung it around her shoulders before helping her stand and asked her what she was talking about. She explained that the big oak was her home tree, but the others nearby were all her offspring. He didn't believe her until she put actions behind her words and melted into the tree leaving only his coat behind.

"Terrified, the young man went to gather the others and told them what he'd just seen. Of course, they didn't believe him, but they followed him to the tree anyhow, and he called out, asking the girl to appear again.

"The crowd gasped as a face appeared in the bark of the tree then pushed outward until a girl stood before them without a stitch on her, just as before. She told these people her story as well, and they came to an agreement with her. She would help protect their land so long as they left her grove in peace.

"With nothing to lose in the deal, the towns folk agreed, and the town of Oak Grove came to be. For years, the woman could be seen around town, helping hunters find the wild game or farmers choose the best places and times to plant. For years, they lived together in peace and prosperity, never discovered by the outside world. But as time passed, the dryad grew tired and eventually faded away, her name forgotten. To this day, no oaks are cut here in Oak Grove, and to this day, this town has prospered."

Betty took a breath, then beamed at her audience. "And there you have it!"

"Thank you," said Tabby. "It's always a joy to hear you tell the story. If you don't mind, I'd like to stay and look a little while longer."

"Take all the time you need." Betty stood from the rocker and patted Tabby's arm. "Just holler if you need anything."

"Will do," Tabby promised.

When the ladies left, Luke grabbed his mother's arm. "Look at this one," he hissed, dragging Tabby to a faded pen and ink drawing.

It was a beautifully detailed sketch of Feya's face staring out of the bark of a tree.

4

At 7 pm on Tuesday evening, the town gathered for a meeting and a vote. At least, those who had been notified about the rushed meeting were there.

Conversations filled the air along with debates and laughter. Neighbors and friends chatted and whispered about those who hadn't shown up.

Frederick Alcroft, the mayor, presided from a low platform and behind a large oak podium, elaborately carved with leaves and acorns. The wood had been salvaged from a tree downed in a storm about a hundred years ago, but the platform was the mayor's addition. He'd have rathered a stage, but there wasn't enough space. It had taken four of the town's burliest men to move the podium, place the platform, then lift the gargantuan piece of art into place.

"Okay folks, quiet down, quiet down!" he called out, waving his hands palm down to emphasize his desire.

"Can everyone hear me?" he asked into the microphone perched in front of him, a folder of notes neatly open. The mic had been his idea as well.

A chorus of yeses rang out.

"Wonderful. Now, as you may know, our town council has been meeting to discuss the idea of developing the grove area."

Cries of outrage lifted around the room, and he made his quieting gesture once more.

"Now, now, just listen a moment," he called over the negative voices, the sound system emitting a squeal of protest. "I'm not talking about the whole grove. The park will be maintained as is, with a few trees thinned to allow for better light, which will lead to better growth. The tourists will still be able to visit our dryad.

"But beyond that is land that is just sitting there with good wood and in prime real-estate. This town will benefit greatly from cutting and developing the unused land. We can still discuss how to use the land itself and what to do with the money the lumber brings in. I'm certain the park would love a stipend to care for the statue and its trees." He paused to take a drink from a plastic bottle that boasted origins of Nordic glaciers.

"The local kids could use a playground as well. We simply haven't had the space for it, but I know plenty of you have asked in the past. We have a whole list of possibilities. In the meantime, we need to vote on having a log company come in and clear the area."

The mayor opened the floor for questions. Hands flew to the air all around the room, and he selected the first by pointing with one manicured finger.

A woman with bright red hair and a stark white coat stood. "So the land would still be available for public use? Or are you going to put in a mall?"

"The intention is for public use. We don't just want development just for the heck of it. This community is growing every day, and our need for enrichment grows with it."

A man in a beat-up Carharrt jacket stood next. "Does this mean taxes will be raised to fund these things?"

"Well yes, but only a negligible amount. The benefits will outweigh the cost." The mayor caught the eye of one of his cronies, who immediately shot his hand into the air. "Yes, Jimmy!"

Jimmy stood. "I, for one, am all for making use of the land. I know my nieces and nephews could use a few good outlets outside of school. If we don't have anything to offer the next generation, they'll just up and leave once they get old enough. This town will shrivel and die with just us old coots living out the rest of our days here. Fresh blood certainly wouldn't hurt either."

"All good points, Jimmy," said the mayor, nodding his head slowly as if the words hadn't originally been his, planned before the meeting began.

The chatter and back and forth continued until every person had the opportunity to voice their opinion if they wanted.

"We'll put it to the vote then. All in favor of bringing in loggers to begin the process, raise your hands for aye."

Hands all over went up.

"The ayes have it! We'll continue with the process and keep you all updated."

"I CANNOT BELIEVE they called a last-minute meeting and I managed to miss the memo," Tabby groused, as she stabbed a Gerber daisy into the arrangement she was working on.

"You wouldn't have liked it," said Sara, doing her

own arranging with a gentler hand. "I only caught the tail end, but the vote went through to clear cut the grove."

"What?!" Tabby shrieked, slamming her scissors point first into the wooden counter so they stood wobbling on their own.

"Yeah, Alcroft put it together in a hurry to keep certain people from hearing and attending."

"Fred-dick," Tabby muttered, yanking her shears free.

"You said it." Sara pointed at her with a deep red dwarf sunflower.

"Who's a dick?" The door opened, and in swaggered Luke. "Morning Mom, just stopping to say how incredibly beautiful, smart, and wonderful you are before I head to school."

"The mayor. What do you want?" Tabby planted her fists on her hips and squinted her eyes in suspicion at her son's compliments.

"To borrow 40 bucks. I'll pay you back as soon as my check hits my account, I promise."

"For what, exactly?" She wasn't going to give up the cash unless he gave a good reason. If he wanted to buy junk, he could wait until payday.

"Uh, Jenny Thompson asked me out. And we were supposed to go out tonight, but her dad is an ass and stole her wallet. And now she's stranded at the gas station because she didn't know her dad took her wallet until now."

Tabby blinked, trying to get her brain to catch up with her son's words. "Okay, so this really has nothing to do with the date you're supposed to go on, but with the fact that you want to be her knight in shining armor, but you already filled our tank. Am I right?"

"Yeah, pretty much." Luke's cheeks reddened.

"And this is the same Jenny Thompson you've been in love with since the 3rd grade?"

"Maaaybe." The red receded as he gave his mother his most charming smile.

"Okay." Tabby snagged her bag from under the counter and pulled out two fifty-dollar bills, handing them to her son. "Go make sure her tank is full. Make sure she has lunch, and make sure she knows if she needs anything at all, not to hesitate to ask. Got it?"

"Yes Mom, thanks. You're the best." He kissed her cheek and tucked the bills into his front pocket.

"No honey, you are. I know you'd have done this even if you weren't finally going on a date with the girl you've been daydreaming about for years, even if it was someone you barely knew or tolerated. You're a good kid."

"Thanks. I'll see you late tonight?"

"Just make sure you text and keep me in the loop, okay?"

He rolled his eyes but grinned anyhow. "Yes, Mom."

After the door closed behind him, Sara turned to Tabby. "Fred-dick isn't the only ass-hat around. Carl Thompson's his runner-up."

"This isn't the first time he's done something like this. The reason Lucas first noticed Jenny was because of a big rip in her winter coat that hadn't been there the day before when they were 9. Carl's behavior has been pretty cagey for years. He went to rehab before Jenny was born, but I'm pretty sure he started using and drinking again."

"Poor kid." Sara frowned, put her work down, and leaned on the counter. "I wish there was more we could do for her."

"Well, maybe we will be able to if things with Lucas works out. He can talk a polar bear into becoming a sun bear. If anyone can get Jenny to call the police on her father, it's him." Tabby tapped a rhythm on the counter.

The front door opened, and both women's heads sprung up to greet the incoming customer.

"Oh, hi, Feya!" Tabby waved her over. "Sara, this is my new neighbor, Feya. Feya, this is my friend, Sara."

"Nice to meet ya." Sara stuck out a hand.

Feya shook it gently. "The pleasure is all mine."

"Nice outfit today," Tabby complimented.

Feya had fashioned high rise dark wash jeans, black ballet flats, and a grey top that revealed just a sliver of her toned stomach.

"Thank you! I think I'm finally getting the hang of it. Why don't you wear this type of clothing?"

"Because I'm old," Tabby said without thinking.

Perplexed, Feya cocked her head to the side. "But I'm so much older than you. Should I not be wearing this?"

"You're fine. You look great. You also look like you're in your twenties."

Sara, clearly lost on the conversation, took a moment to study both women. "Okay, I'm confused. Feya, if you don't mind me asking, if you're not in your 20's, how old are you?"

Feya lifted her eyes up and to the right as she attempted to calculate. "Oh, at least 700, give or take a decade or two."

Sara's eyebrows rose. "Uh, what?"

"Would you give us a moment, Sara?" Tabby danced out from behind the counter, grabbed Feya's arm, and tugged her out the door.

"Feya, are you going to tell everyone in town what you are?"

She shrugged. "I don't see why not. I am what I am. There's no hiding it."

"But are you sure? People are going to think you're nuts."

Feya's eyebrows rose and scrunched together. "But I do grow acorns." She pulled one out of her pocket and displayed it between her thumb and forefinger. "See?"

"No, I mean they're going to think you're insane. Mad or whatever."

The confusion didn't leave her face. "Hm. Well, I'll just have to keep showing people the truth until they have to believe."

Tabby's jaw dropped. "Uh, that's a plan, I guess."

"Good. Thank you. Shall we go talk to your friend now?"

Feya made her way back to the front door and let herself in, leaving Tabby outside.

Tabby knew with no uncertainty that Feya was telling the truth, but she was worried about how people would treat her. Ancient though she might be, she was still so innocent and naive.

The door opened again, then banged closed behind Sara, who followed Feya's lead.

"—here, watch me." Feya disappeared into a tree in front of her new audience.

Moments later, Tabby and Sara were back inside, working in silence, Feya having taken off to do whatever it was dryads did.

"So, what are we going to do?" Sara asked after putting the finishing touches on her work.

"What do you mean?"

"Well, the town's planning on bulldozing her grove. Don't you think she'd want to know something like that?"

"Good point. I'm not sure how she's going to take it though. She's... um... different."

"Of course, she is. She's a dryad." Sara paused, biting her lip. "Dryads are real."

"Yup and yup."

"My mind is kind of blown right now, and I'm kind of wondering if I'm the crazy one." Sara took a sip of her water and put her tools away.

"Well, if you're crazy, then I'm also crazy, and so is Luke… and I'm guessing a good chunk of the town will be before too long.

5

Feya stood next to the computer, intent on Luke's latest lesson. This was modern development she approved of: every bit of knowledge, right at your fingertips, if only you asked the right questions. He explained how to plug key information into a search engine, which now brought up legends featuring dryads.

"I was around for quite some time, how is it that not a single person wrote about me?" She frowned, then bit her lip as she read down the list of links.

"Well, they did, they just didn't post it online." Lucas leaned back in his seat and crossed his arms over his chest, letting Feya skim through the articles on her own.

"So, you can't find *everything* then." Her brow furrowed in disappointment.

"No, not everything. We could write your story ourselves and put it out there if you really want," he offered, knowing plenty of ways to share the story, but also knowing that's all it ever would be.

It would never fully represent the creature standing next to him dressed in a crop top and jeans.

Feya rolled her chair to the side to address him. "Not just yet. Where is the story then?"

"Huh?" Lucas lost their conversation as he read the Wikipedia article she'd left off on.

"My story. How did you learn it? Who tells it?"

"Well, so, you saw your statue, right? Up the road from there is the historical society. There's a whole room there dedicated to your legend. They have a stack of booklets for whoever and lots of art work. There's a really good one of your face done with pen and ink."

Feya's face lit up. "Oh yes! I remember sitting for that. I can't remember his name, it was so long ago, but he did a lot more than one drawing. He probably took the rest of them with him since they were far more intimate. He had a lot of opportunity the winter I spent in his bed."

"Whoa!" Luke held up his hand. "TMI! I don't need those details, lady."

She cocked her head. "What's TMI?"

He blinked. "Man, you have a lot to learn. It means too much information."

"I thought it was quite the right amount." Her eyebrows scrunched, confused by this young being's assessment of her words.

"I still didn't need to know." He covered the sides of his head with large palms. "My delicate, childlike ears."

"Oh, psh. It's not like you're a virgin." Feya rolled her eyes at him, then halted her movement as she watched red take over his face, starting at the tips of his ears.

"You are a virgin? How can that be? Everything on the computer states that modern men are not virgins."

"Please stop." Luke muttered, then turned to face her. "First off, I'm only 17, so not legally a man yet. And just because pop culture says something doesn't mean it's the truth."

Feya leaned over and sniffed him. "You do smell faintly of a female, but not strong enough to have swapped bodily fluids."

"And that's enough of that." Tabby breezed into the room and grabbed Feya's arm to tug her away from her beet red son and into the kitchen.

"What? What did I say wrong this time?" Feya asked, confused, as Tabby pulled out a chair for her.

Tabby sighed and raked her fingers through her hair. "It wasn't wrong, per se. Just kind of rude. Sniffing people isn't exactly a common practice. Neither is commenting on their sex lives."

"But all those magazines on the coffee table—" Feya started.

Tabby held up a hand to stop her. "Contradict every-thing I'm saying, I know. That's just media. It's not real life."

"They're real people, aren't they?" Feya chewed her lip, her eyebrows furrowing.

"Yes but—"

"Then it's real life."

"It's rumors at best. Feya, I really need to talk to you about something important."

Feya waited, her face smoothing.

The human sighed, and twirled a strand of hair around her finger. "Okay. So, something bad is happening in this town." She pursed her lips, trying to come up with how best to approach the subject.

"Oh, I know. That's why I woke up in the first place. There were some disgusting men galumphing through my grove talking about killing my family."

"Yes, well, now it's more than just talk. They voted on it the other day, and they're reaching out to logging companies now." She paused, Feya's words sinking in. "Did you just call the mayor disgusting?"

"I did. He and his friends were groping the statue and talking about rutting around the woods with me."

"Gross. I'm so sorry you heard that." Tabby shuddered in disgust and sympathy, laying a gentle hand on her new friend's shoulder.

Feya shrugged. "It's nothing I haven't heard before. Men have always had strange reactions to the fae, especially dryads like me. The myths got that part correct."

Tabby shuddered again.

"Anyway, that's why I came to you for help. I knew no one would take me seriously if I looked different and behaved strangely, but I've got to put a stop to this by any means necessary," Feya snarled, slamming an open palm on the counter.

Tabby jumped at the noise. "Well, why don't you start by talking to them first, before you resort to more drastic measures."

"Very well. When will they be meeting again?"

"Soon, I'd assume. They want to discuss what to do with the land once it's cleared."

"Well, I can answer that," said Feya darkly. "They're going to leave it the hell alone or pay more than they're willing to give."

"Whoa there, ya blood thirsty critter." Luke joined them in the kitchen, having finally settled his blushing. He was unused to being the one that blushed as it was always his goal to get others to do it instead. Typically, it was only his mom that could pull it off, but Feya seemed to have a special knack for it.

"Oh, by the way, how did your date go the other night?" Tabby switched subjects to something less life threatening.

"I'd say it went well. Like I said, I can smell her on him." Feya's face brightened with a smile, happy for her young friend.

"Feya, why don't you go for a walk and clear your mind. I think I'd rather talk to my son alone."

Feya giggled and exited through the back door.

"She knew exactly what she was doing that time, didn't she?" Tabby sighed and leaned back in her seat.

Chuckling, Luke nodded. "She seems so young and innocent, but she's really not, is she?"

"No. Not even a little."

FEYA'S WALK took her downtown, where she could people watch and look in the windows of the various shops. Giggling groups of teens gathered around the benches, while adults strolled in couples or alone.

The soft thunk of sneakers heading in her direction made her pause and turn.

Sara trotted straight for her, ponytail swinging.

"Feya! I was hoping I could catch you. I wanted to talk to you."

"Oh, okay." Feya drew to a stop, waiting to hear what she had to say.

"Well, not right here. Let's go to the Sip Down and have something warm to drink." Sara linked their elbows, drawing her farther down the street.

"Oh, I don't have any money." Feya extracted her arm gently.

"No worries, it's my treat. Now come on, woman." Sara reattached herself and set a brisk pace down the road.

Feya wasn't about to argue. Besides, she wanted as

many friends as possible on her side before it became time for action.

They entered the little coffee shop which shared a wall with the bar next door. Bill owned the coffee shop while his sister, Bev, owned Beverley's Brew House. Their businesses were separated by an accordion-like partition that covered a gap above a half wall which they opened during the evenings when there was live entertainment.

The two women selected their drinks and split a cinnamon coffee roll the size of Feya's head.

"Okay, so, hopefully Tabby's told you about the meeting about the grove." She paused to take a bite while Feya nodded.

"Well, they're having another meeting tonight, and I think maybe you should speak in opposition. You should get a chance to plead your case."

Feya nodded. "I like you. You're up front and you support my cause. I can't ask for more than that." She took a tentative sip of her steaming mint tea.

"Thanks! I try to be honest, but even if I didn't, my face would give me away." She whipped out a tiny note-book. "Let's get something together so you can keep your thoughts organized. How are you going to start off? Are you going to reveal what you are? Talk about historical pride? You should be assertive but relatable. Ease them into things. What's our angle?" Sara stuck the end of the pen in her mouth as her mind whirred with ideas.

FEYA GOT ready for the meeting at Sara's house, with every intention of getting together with Tabby beforehand.

"Do I really look okay?" Feya studied herself in the mirror. The French braid hanging down her spine and her glamour were tailored according to what Sara deemed professionally stylish. She tugged at the hem of her peacock blue peplum top. Paired with black skinny jeans and another pair of ballet flats, it was far more conservative than what she had been wearing. Of course, there was a certain teenage boy who had given her most of her fashion advice.

"You look great. Young, sexy, and fun is fine around town, but if you're going to be talking business, you need to dress seriously." Sara swiped a light lip stain over her own mouth, sharing the mirror with her guest.

Feya pulled the end of the braid over her shoulder and fiddled with the ends. "Okay, I trust you."

A loud knock interrupted them.

"That had better be Tabby!" Sara dashed out to answer it.

Soft female voices flitted to Feya's ears, confirming that it was indeed Tabby. Without another glance at the mirror, she joined her allies, ready to face her enemies.

THE MEETING WAS CALLED to order over the chatter of the town residents. It took them a moment to settle down, even as Mayor Alcott waved his hands in his signature simmer-down motion.

"All right, folks, all right. There's a lot on the agenda today, so we need to get started and stay on track." He began droning on about budgets, school fundraisers, and the upcoming tourist season.

Feya jangled her legs in anticipation, clutching the notebook with the notes Sara had taken for her in the Sip Down.

"You might as well relax. Mayor Fred-dick isn't going

to open the floor until he's run out of air," Sara advised, keeping her voice soft to not be overheard.

Feya had been still for a couple hundred years, but now, when so much was at stake, she found it difficult.

After what felt like hours, the mayor closed his agenda. "All right friends, you have the floor. Any questions? Suggestions?"

Feya bounded to her feet, unable to wait any longer. "I have something to say." Her voice rang out over all the others.

The mayor frowned. "Do you live in Oak Grove, young lady?" he asked, inspecting her face.

"Yes, as I have for the last several hundred years," she stated bluntly.

Tittering spread over the hall.

The mayor chuckled along with them. "No really, do you live here? I don't think I can place your face. It does look familiar though."

"Well, if you've visited the Dryad room at the historical society, it should. My face is there quite a bit. I'm told an old lover of mine left a rather accurate pen and ink of me."

"Feya," Tabby hissed. "I think maybe you should start somewhere else…"

Feya ignored her friend, and pressed on. "We had a deal, this town and I. You leave my grove in peace, and in turn, I help ensure this town prospers. Have I not followed through on my word?" She spread her arms open. "Of course, I have. Look at this beautiful village. Why then have you chosen to violate the agreement?"

"The dryad is just a fairy tale." The mayor slammed a hand down on the podium." You can't expect us to believe you're a day over 23, never mind hundreds of years old. Please concede the floor and quit interrupting this meeting." He pointed toward the back of the room. "If you are not one of my citizens, you may listen, but you may not interfere."

"It is you that are my citizens. I was here long before any man planted a field. And I shall be here long after you're dead." Feya's voice lowered into something less than human.

Sara squeaked, and tapped her on the leg. "That's definitely not in our notes, Feya."

"This was funny at first, but I think it's time for you to leave, young lady." The mayor clutched the podium, his knuckles whitening, even as his face turned red. No one had spoken so disrespectfully to him in years. Yet here was this stranger telling lies and tall tales.

"Oh, I know it's not funny. Every oak in this town is my family. You harm a single one of them, you harm me, and I will not stand by and let it happen."

"Um, Feya, let's go get some fresh air." Sara stood and attempted to tug Feya out of the auditorium.

Tabby stood as well, gently taking her other arm.

"Yes, ladies, please think twice before bringing delusional friends to town meetings," Frederic sneered.

"I am not delusional," Feya hissed. "I am the dryad of Oak Grove and you will not harm my trees!"

Laughter followed Feya out of the building as tears streaked down her face.

Once outside, Feya collapsed on the front steps. "Why won't they listen?"

"Because they're ignorant greedy men who only care about their bank accounts." Tabby sat beside her. "Even if there was a tree in the middle of that room for you to disappear into, I don't think they would have listened." She gently rubbed her new friend's back as she sobbed. "We won't quit trying, I promise. We just need to find another way."

6

Fredrick Alcroft paced his office, raging, after the town meeting concluded.

"Can you believe the audacity of that child? Who does she think she is, trying to stop us? Stupid fucking tree hugger. It's not like we're tearing out all the trees. We're leaving the ones in the park area."

"I know darling." Mary, his diminutive and plump wife attempted to sooth him. "Come have a glass of whisky with me. She didn't cause any real harm."

"Not yet, just wait until she gets all her little hippy friends to stage a protest, tie themselves to the log truck or some bull shit like that."

"We'll deal with it as it comes. You can't make everyone happy. you know that." Mary pulled out two short glasses and added two fingers of liquor from an antique bottle. She handed one to her husband and sipped the other herself.

"You're just the perfect wife, you know that, Mary?" he asked, taking a seat on the little couch.

"I try," she said, sliding one hand up his slacks on his thigh. "How about I help take your mind off it."

Her hand traveled further, unbuttoning and unzipping his pants, before kneeling before him, her knees crackling as she moved.

"Just think. When this is over, maybe she'll be kneeling before you too. She is a pretty little thing."

"That she is." the mayor sucked in a breath, his imagination racing as his wife fueled the fantasy.

THE NEXT MORNING, while reading the paper and drinking his coffee, Fredrick decided to call a little meeting with his inner circle. Maybe they'd have some ideas about how to deal with his little problem. He pulled out his phone and shot out a quick email.

That evening, Fred and his pals sat around his kitchen table drinking beers.

Mary bustled in with a tray laden with snacks. "Is there anything else I can get for you boys?" she asked.

Fred slapped and squeezed his wife's round bottom. "Nothing I care to share with these bastards. Why don't you go get into something nice, and we can continue last night's conversation when we're done."

Mary flushed, and hurried out of the room. She hated how crass Fred talked when he was with his friends. She didn't mind such things in private, but the last thing she wanted was to have images of her in those men's minds. She put up with it because she loved her husband, and it thrilled her that he still wanted her, even if he needed the occasional tease from something younger and firmer. She even enjoyed the tease herself from time to time, though he would never accept another man in their bedroom.

He'd told her it was like when a prize stallion needed a tease mare to prepare him for the act.

He was lying of course. It was the mare that was teased in a breeding program, not the stallion. But he knew she'd never find out the truth on her own.

The men laughed as the door closed behind her, and Fred called their attention to the issue at hand.

"So. That little girl at the meeting last night. We can't have riff raff like that throwing wrenches in our plans," he said, taking a long pull from his bottle.

"You said it. These hippy tree huggers think they own the world. The only thing a girl like that is good for is—" the man grabbed the hair on an imaginary head and shoved it at his crotch.

"Now, now, Roger. We all know your preferences, but this isn't the time for that. That's your private business. Right now, we need to discuss what to do about her. Despite all her crazy talk, some people were actually listening to her. People around town are talking about town history and town pride. We need to get their minds out of the past and launch them forward into the future. Suggestions?"

"Cut some trees down and watch her disappointment when nothing happens?" Jimmy suggested, sticking his pencil behind his ear.

"Funny perhaps, but not the best **PR** maneuver." Fred shook his head.

"What about getting some really beautiful plans drawn up and putting together some numbers so people will see the benefits. Right now, it's just an idea in their heads. We need them to see the possibilities," another man stated and the others nodded.

"Very good points. Are you willing to start putting together a presentation? I've got my notes all organized; I can get them to you after the meeting is over." Fred leaned forward, liking what he was hearing.

The men tossed several more ideas back and forth and came up with a plan they were convinced would be the ticket to gaining back public favor on the project.

Several beers later, the discussion turned back to Feya.

"Do you think she actually lives in the woods? And really thinks she's a dryad?" Jimmy asked, rocking his chair back on two legs.

"She sure sounded convincing," said Roger. "Or maybe that was just her rack." He mimed squeezing a pair of breasts.

Raucous laughter filled the room at that comment.

"I bet she's a wild one in the sack. All the crazy ones are," Jimmy remarked.

"Too true," Fred agreed. "I wouldn't mind taking her for a ride either."

"Would Mary be amenable to that?" Another man asked, raising his eyebrows. He'd been under the impression that the mayor's marriage was a happy and passionate one.

"Oh, it was her idea," Fred lowered his voice and leaned in. "I was pretty ticked off after last night's meeting."

"Rightly so!" said Jimmy.

Fred nodded. "Thank you. Well, Mary, luscious Mary, made me a drink and decided to take my mind off of things. You should have heard the things she said, but the one that sticks out most in my mind is her suggestion that maybe that girl would be kneeling before me one day, like she was."

"Oh, damn!" Jimmy slammed his hand on the table. "That's sexy. Who knew little Mary had it in her."

"She's a spicy one. She definitely goes out of the way to

keep me satisfied." Fred thrust his hips up from his seat in emphasis. "Wish you all had a girl like Mary."

"Well, she does seem to be into sharing—"

"Don't finish that statement, Roger. Mary is mine. You keep your filthy hands off her."

Roger held up his hands. "All right, all right. Man, I think I'm going to Beverly's after this. I need to get laid something awful."

"Yeah, you do."

They talked more about conquests from their past, and the encounters they hoped to have in the future. Many included Feya. Because she was right – there was just something about Dryads that men just couldn't resist. It was their power and their horror.

7

Though Ethan Brady had never been to Oak Grove before, he had heard of it. Folklore was one of his favorite things, and the fact that there was supposedly a dryad in those woods was part of the reason he'd signed on for the job. Of course, he had no idea what he'd do if he actually found one. He couldn't exactly participate in decimating the sacred grove of a tree spirit.

There wasn't much information on her, and he was eager to hear the legend from locals. It was a long drive from home, so he'd opted to rent a room in one of the three hotels Oak Grove boasted. Well, one hotel, one motel, and a bed and breakfast. His room was in the hotel.

He enjoyed logging. Spending his days outside and decent pay were what initially attracted him to the job. His boss, Brian Whitley, was an okay person to work for; sometimes cranky, but usually fair.

Growing up on the Pleasant Point Passamaquoddy Reservation on the coast of Maine, Ethan hadn't had much opportunity to travel. Now, he was getting paid to do it. It wasn't that he didn't love his mother's people or his former home, but a change of scenery was nice now and then. With a father who had been an outsider, he never truly felt he belonged.

He never met his father's parents. From what he knew, his father had simply shown up in town one day and he and his mother became inseparable the moment they laid eyes on each other. Ethan had asked about his grandparents a time or two, but his dad had given him sad smiles and told him they weren't around anymore.

His maternal grandparents had welcomed Ethan's father, and treated him like their own from the very beginning. His father and grandfather had spent hours together talking about history, culture, and what it was to be a part of the family. They'd both passed on their ideals of kindness, respect, and thoughtfulness to Ethan.

The cottage he'd grown up in was put to shame by the large, well kept houses that lined the roads heading to the heart of the town. Most boasted beautiful gardens in full bloom, despite the early date.

"Maybe it's because of the dryad," he chuckled to himself as he pulled into the hotel's nearly empty parking lot. He supposed it was a bit early in the year for tourists to take over the little town. Either way, he'd gotten a decent rate on his room.

At the front desk, he got his reservation sorted and accepted his key card, which he pushed into his wallet before returning it to his back pocket.

"Enjoy your stay!" said the receptionist, leaning bent arms on the counter and pushing the top of her cleavage up and out of her shirt. "Don't hesitate to ask if you need anything." She looked him up and down, from his short dark hair, warm bronze skin tone, sliding over his toned body. "Anything at all." She licked her lips.

"Uh, thanks?" He turned quickly and headed for the

elevator, feeling extremely uncomfortable. Hard labor and hours in the gym had given him a lean, strong body, but deep down, he'd always be that shy scrawny kid who never got picked first in gym class.

While he did want female companionship, the receptionist simply didn't spark a response in him.

Ethan found his room and tossed his bag on one of the beds before pulling out his phone to call his boss.

"Hey, Brady!" Brian answered after the first ring. "I take it you made it okay."

"Yeah." Ethan pulled his charger out and plugged it into the wall. "It was further than I thought though. How come we traveled so far?"

"Because the mayor is in a hurry to get this project done and is willing to pay for it. I just got a call from the big guy and it seems they're having trouble with a tree hugger who insists that the grove is her home. So please keep your inner weirdo in check."

Ethan stilled, clutching the phone. "Oh?"

"Yeah, guess she's bat shit crazy. Glad he warned us. But anyway, we don't want them thinking you're one of them."

"Brian, you're an ass." Ethan glared at the room, since he couldn't glare at his boss.

"Yeah well, I'm just saying."

"Goodbye, Brian. I'll see you tomorrow." Ethan hung up the phone and tossed it next to his bag. "Jackass," he muttered, heading out.

He was going to tour the town to find out more about the Oak Grove Dryad and if they should really be worried about the girl. Something deep within told him not to mess with this place, to leave it alone, that this girl might just be the real deal, but it was just a gut feeling. He'd have to meet her before he'd be able to tell for sure. Of course, if she was the dryad, then he'd be stuck trying how to figure out how to stop his job.

He took the stairs down and did his best to avoid the lobby. The receptionist might be a nice girl, but she definitely wasn't his type. Not that he had any idea what his type was.

"Maybe someone with a little mystery," he muttered, darting out the door before she could look up from her computer.

He quickly located the Grove Diner in one of the many renovated older homes, which was easily overlooked if not for the sign out front. He tucked into his food and people-watched the townies strolling down the sidewalk.

A pair of women caught his eye as they approached. Both appeared younger than Ethan's 32 years, with their trendy clothes; faces and hair free from signs of age. He hadn't found any grays on his head, but he had developed a few wrinkles from hours spent out of doors.

One was full of animation and laughter, but it was her companion that made Ethan's heart stutter in his chest. As she drew closer, there was something about how she carried herself that spoke of years of poetic motion, like a breeze dancing through new spring leaves. Maybe she wasn't as young as he'd thought.

He blinked as they entered the dinner and seated themselves closer to the counter.

"Sir, would you like any more coffee?" His waitress, a middle-aged woman with short curly blonde hair, brought him back to himself.

"Oh, no thank you. I'm good with this." He covered the white mug with his palm. It was still half full, as was his plate.

"Anything else I can get you, honey?" she asked.

Ethan shook his head and let his eyes wander to the

most fascinating creature he'd ever seen. Her skin was pale while her shoulders, the bridge of her nose, and her clavicle sported the bright red of a sunburn. She looked like she'd lived in the shade her entire life, though the undertones of her skin betrayed a warmer tone that might be gained.

Her brown hair was so long it reached the swell of her denim-clad rear. Her body, though lean and strong, was softened by gentle curves.

He let his eyes wander, drinking in the sight of her. If anyone in this little town was a dryad, it was her.

She laughed at something her friend said, tossing her head back and sending her hair rippling in waves. She put a hand to her stomach like the joke was too much to handle, then clutched her friend's shoulder with the other. As their food was delivered, he got a hold of himself, finished his meal, and paid, leaving the waitress a generous tip for putting up with his absent-mindedness.

What kind of creep was he, staring at a woman like that? If he saw a guy staring at his little sister like this, he'd be sorely tempted to break the guy's nose. He'd done it once, though the guy had approached Sophie for more than a look.

His sister had been so angry with him for interfering when the guy wouldn't back off. She told him she could handle herself. He'd known she could—they'd both taken kickboxing since they were little—but he was her big brother. She hadn't bought that answer either, calling him a neanderthal.

He shook his head, chuckling at the memory. That had been years ago. She'd left right after she finished college and moved to Florida. Now he only saw her on holidays, if he was lucky.

Hoping to catch another glimpse of the otherworldly beauty from the previous night, Ethan had breakfast at the same diner the next morning. He enjoyed his eggs, sausage, and toast but left without a sighting.

He pretended not to hear the receptionist on his way back to his room, and then again on his way back out.

A few minutes later, he pulled into the parking lot of Oak Grove Park, the tourist attraction set up to honor the dryad, and headed for the worksite.

"Hey there, you ready to get started?" Brian slapped his shoulder in friendly greeting then motioned him to begin unpacking equipment.

A carved statue stood sentinel over the park, and Ethan took a moment to study it. Her body was coated in a blanket of moss that looked very much like a dress. Perhaps an artsy local had tried their hand at moss painting.

"Hello!" An emphatic male voice yanked him from his thoughts.

Ethan turned to view the older gentleman.

"I'm Fredrick Alcroft, mayor of this little slice of heaven." The man rocked up on his toes, as if to gain height

"Nice to meet you, sir." Ethan held out his hand in greeting.

The mayor's hands were soft, and he barely gripped Ethan's hand as he shook it once.

Brian strode over to introduce himself and motioned for the others to join them.

"I just wanted to give you a rough sketch of the area." Alcroft handed some papers over to Brian, who shoved them under his arm to look at later. "And to remind you that there's a young woman that's been causing problems.

Bit of a tree hugger. If she gives you any trouble, don't hesitate to call the cops. She's either delusional or just plain full of bull crap." He chuckled and shook his head.

"There's always a handful of those around. Especially for a project like this," Brian jutted his thumb over his shoulder. "I'm sure we'll handle her just fine."

"Good, good. I just wanted to give you a heads up. If you boys need anything, don't hesitate to call my office." The mayor tucked his thumbs in his slack pockets.

"Will do. See you around, Mr. Mayor," said Brian, pulling the paper from under his arm and using it to salute the older man.

"I look forward to it." Alcroft strutted towards his car, opened the door, and scraped the bottom of his loafers on the frame before driving away.

"That guy gives off creeper vibes, or is it just me?" Ethan asked one of his coworkers as he hauled a bright orange tripod into the woods.

"It's not just you. It's probably the oil of politics coating him," he answered, hefting his equipment on his shoulder.

Ethan turned his gaze back to the statue. "Maybe."

As lunch break rolled around, Ethan set aside his equipment and rolled his shoulders. He'd been doing a lot of hunching while surveying the area.

His work boots crunched over old leaves as he made his way out of the woods and marveled over the fact that the entire forest was oaks. There wasn't a single spruce or birch in sight, and underbrush was the only other vegetation. He could certainly see why a legend had sprung up here, and he found it a shame that they'd be cutting most of it down.

Ahead, he heard voices, one being his boss and the other belonging to a young woman.

"I'm sorry ma'am, but this is the job we've been hired to do," said Brian, clearly trying to sound sympathetic.

"Don't you get it? This is my home. Mine. It doesn't belong to the town. The grove belongs to me. Being asleep for the last couple hundred years doesn't change that." The musical alto of the woman's words sent shivers down Ethan's spine.

"I'm afraid the paperwork says otherwise. These woods are well within the town lines."

Ethan wove his way through a few more trees before the woman came into view. Her back was to him, but he recognized the long chocolate hair from the diner.

"What's up?" Ethan asked, approaching the pair.

Brian stepped back from the girl. "I believe this is the young lady the mayor mentioned earlier."

"Hello," Ethan said, holding his hand out to her. "I'm Ethan."

She was slow to reach out and grip his calloused hand with her long elegant fingers, her eyes distrustful. "Feya."

"Feya, I'm about to take my lunch break. Why don't you join me and you can tell me about the grove and see if we can't sort this out." Her fingers were surprisingly rough, and she smelled of sunshine and growing things. He had to fight against his instinct to step closer, to touch that silken sheet of hair.

She looked into his eyes, and he felt as if she was studying his soul.

"My treat," he added, gently letting go of her fingers, then clenching them at the memory of how good they'd felt against his own.

"Alright then. Listening is a good start, I suppose.

That's what Tabby tells me anyhow," she said and turned with him.

"Who's Tabby?" he asked, shoving his hands in his pockets so he could resist taking hers again.

"She runs the flower shop and has been my teacher. Sort of. When I woke up, I was so far behind on things." She smiled at him. "Would you like to meet her?"

"Uh, maybe later, okay? I've only got 45 minutes for lunch." He grinned down at her, then knit his brow in confusion. "Wait, did you say the last couple hundred years?"

"Yes, I did. I'm the Oak Grove dryad. I was awake for the founding of the town, but things were going so well that I decided to take a little rest. A little more time passed than I intended." She grinned in a way that was almost feline.

"Huh," was all he could think of to say. His intuition told him to believe her, but how could it be true?

His subconscious sprang forward, whispering in his ear, telling him not to be an idiot.

Feya frowned and slowed her pace. "You don't believe me, do you?"

He stopped and stared down into her upturned face, her green eyes pulling him in. Before he could drown, he swallowed, and started forward again. "I don't know yet. Is the diner okay for lunch?"

She fell back into step with him. "Sure. I went there for breakfast, but I like the food."

She had? How had he missed her?

That inner voice whispered, *because you're an idiot.*

He scratched his ear. "Good. That's good."

The rest of their walk was silent, each lost in their own thoughts.

Ethan stepped forward as they reached the diner, and

held the door open for Feya. They found themselves an empty booth then ordered from the cheery waitress. Their silence dragged on.

"So are you really a dryad?" he asked finally, not knowing what else to say.

"I really am. I had an agreement with the first settlers to never touch my grove, and in return, I would do everything I could to assure the town prospered. They held to their word until now. They've forgotten the old ways; forgotten the fae that lived on these lands long before they ever settled here."

"I can understand that. My mother's family has lots of stories about the old spirits. I've never encountered one before, though." While his mind was telling him to remain skeptical, he couldn't ignore his instincts or his meddling grandmother.

The waitress set down their meals and stepped away without interrupting.

"Well now you have." Feya told him about the friendships she had formed with the Oak Grove residence during her earlier days with them and of the new friends since waking up, about the town meeting, and about the mayor's cruel words.

"It's my grove, and I *will* defend it. Mark my words. When the first tree is felled, this town will feel my wrath." She stabbed at her salad.

Ethan was inclined to believe her. Whether she was truly the dryad or not, she was definitely something supernatural.

8

Over the next week, Feya saw Ethan several more times, though she didn't get a chance to talk to him.

The crew he worked with continued hiking with their strange instruments all around her territory. They tied orange plastic ribbons around her trees, marking each phase of their project.

Feya paced deep into the forest, far from the commotion, then called her little chickadee friend to her.

She heard his song before she spotted him and held out a finger for him to perch on.

"Would you mind doing me a favor?" she asked, giving a gentle stroke to his feathery breast.

Chick-ah-deehehehe! he responded, fluffing his feathers then nibbling her fingertips.

"Can you determine how much land they've covered? They tied plastic to trees to mark their boundaries."

Dee-dee-dee! He took flight, and Feya watched him disappear through the trees. A little bird wouldn't be noticed by anyone. She'd learned that chickadees were the Maine state bird from the town's website, and they were incredibly common. She'd made Luke show her the state on a map and its relation to its neighbors. The world was much bigger than she'd realized.

Her keen ears picked up the sounds of chickadees calling to one another and the fluttering of many tiny wings.

A female chipmunk darted to her, planting her front paws on Feya's bare ankle.

"Hello there!" she said, kneeling down. She reached into the pocket of her forest green dress and pulled out a handful of sunflower seeds she'd begged Tabby for earlier that day.

"I THINK my friends would love some of these!" She grabbed a few of the salted seeds from a plastic sack on the counter that Luke had deposited earlier.

"You're friends?" Tabby asked, her eyebrows raising.

"The creatures that live in the grove: birds, squirrels."

"Oh! I'll be right back." Tabby disappeared down the hall while Feya sucked the salt off the seeds before chewing them. Unlike these strange humans, she ate them hull and all.

"Here." Tabby deposited a half full plastic bag on the table filled with unsalted seeds. "We feed the birds all year round, but I only toss out sunflower seeds during the winter. You're certainly welcome to them."

"Thank you so much!" She clutched the sack to her chest.

THE CHIPMUNK STUFFED the seeds into her cheek pouches then dashed up the fabric covering Feya's legs, and disappeared into her pocket, where she continued shoving seeds in her mouth.

"It's spring, little one. You don't need to start hoarding quite yet." She gave the pocket a gentle tap with her index finger.

The chipmunk reemerged and chittered at her, then dashed a few feet away and paused to look at Feya and twitch her tail, as if expecting to be followed.

"Okay, you lead on."

Several trees away, the little chipmunk dove into a hole and was gone for a couple minutes before reemerging with a tiny wriggling pink creature clutched in her teeth.

"Oh, I see!" Feya exclaimed, laying both her hands over her heart. "You need more variety than that."

She snaked her fingers into her other pocket and withdrew a large handful of acorns. She set them just before the mouth of the burrow, inches away from the mother and her offspring.

"I'll leave you to it then."

She stood just as a flock of chickadees came to rest on a branch, chattering animatedly.

"Okay, okay. One at a time."

One chickadee took off through the trees, followed by another, and then another, until all the birds were in the air winding their way through the trees in a wild conga line.

Something was amiss.

Her human clothing slid into nothingness, leaving her clad in her true form: brown skin bare to the afternoon breeze. Her hair was a wild mass of twigs, leaves, and moss. She touched the nearest oak and was immediately accepted into its embrace.

She became a breath on the wind. Flitting from limb to

limb in astral form, following the birds' excited path. Before long, the sound of diesel engines grated her ears along with the pungency of spent fuel. Male voices were buried under the roar of the machinery as they approached the edge of her grove. She settled halfway up an oak, just behind the statue, and separated herself, bringing her body back into the open air. She crept down the limb, her fingers sinking into the bark and wood in perfect symbiosis.

The men she'd seen moving through her trees earlier were all there, standing around, drinking beers and sodas out of cans. She spotted Ethan's dark hair and leaned out towards him. He was dressed in bright orange chaps with leather gloves covering his hands, and he clutched a helmet under one arm. One of the other men was signaling a massive truck into place. Another unloaded a machine that sported huge arms. Chainsaws waited at attention, lined up on the tailgate of a pickup truck.

She craned farther, confident that her natural body would remain camouflaged to anyone who wasn't paying close attention to her current perch. A stout man of middling height took a chart from inside one of the trucks, along with a can of spray paint, and began marking trees. She noted the selection was aimed at thinning out the area with a smattering of young and old trees.

Another vehicle showed up, and Mayor Alcroft exited wearing a shiny new construction helmet, then rounded his vehicle and opened the passenger side door. Mary stepped out, also wearing a brand-new safety helmet, and grasped her husband's fingers.

Other cars appeared bearing more of Oak Grove's citizens, as if this were something to be celebrated. Many had their phones out taking photos while one set up a professional looking camera and began taking shot after shot. A fork truck and a few other pieces of equipment rolled forward and drew all the attention as they began moving the statue.

It was first carefully wrapped and padded around the bottom half then lifted from the ground, where it had sunk surprisingly deep over the years. It was driven to the middle of the lot, settled on a wooden pallet, then roped off. No one wanted the beautiful piece of art to get damaged. It was their main tourist attraction, after all.

Ethan stood at the edge of the clearing, inches away from the tree Feya rested in, frowning.

Soundlessly, she made her way to the ground, and when she was certain there were no eyes pointed in her direction, she slapped a rough hand over Ethan's mouth and dragged him back into the trees.

He struggled but was no match to the strength of an ancient oak as she hauled him farther and farther from the noise of the crowd.

At last, she released him and stepped away.

He spun to face his attacker, his body tense with fear.

As he watched, Feya pulled on her human glamour. The rough texture of bark smoothed into blemish-free skin. Harsh green hair turned brown and silky. The illusion of the green dress she'd been wearing earlier flowed over her form. Dumbfounded, he dropped to his knees before her.

"I saw the equipment. Do you truly plan to continue with this?" she hissed, her eyes narrowed and her muscles tense.

The dryad's true form was like nothing Ethan had ever seen before. She was the most beautiful creature he'd ever laid eyes on; even more beautiful than this human face she now wore.

"Ethan?" she noted his expression and dropped down

to his level, taking his gloved hands in her own. She hadn't noticed he'd lost his helmet when she'd hauled him away from his people.

His eyes snapped to hers. "You're really a dryad." He reached toward her but didn't make contact.

"Yes," she said, grabbing his hand again and resting it against her cheek.

"So you're really hundreds of years old?" he asked, pulling up taller on his knees and bringing up his other hand to cup the other side of her face, stroking her cheeks with his thumbs.

"I really am." She touched his face in return. "These trees are all descended from my primogenial oak. They are my offspring and also parts of my whole." She drew in closer, as his breath caught and his heart raced.

Feya stiffened, her eyes flew wide, and she fought for breath.

He dropped his hands, thinking he'd done something wrong.

Her body flew backwards then hit the ground with a thud, and he knew it wasn't something he'd done. As her head lifted up and back and her body bowed away from the ground, inhuman sounds ripped from her throat.

As she continued to scream, her glamour fell away once more, and the ground shifted. Roots burst through the soil underfoot and wrapped around her, steadying her, and lifting her upright.

Ethan ran forward but was halted as a branch slammed into his chest.

Sap gushed from Feya's eyes and out of her nose, her body snapped, and her screams grew until he had to cover his ears or risk his eardrums bursting. The skin at her shins split upwards and more sap spurted, covering her feet. The roots wrapped around her, and there was no telling where her feet began and the roots ended as they protected her as well as they could. Ethan was forced back again, and while he could no longer see her, her shrieks still rang clear. The sight and sound of her pain was seared into his memories forever.

He turned and ran, following the path left when Feya had dragged him in. Trees pushed him forward, towards his crew. As he lifted his helmet from the ground where he'd first been grabbed, a tree cracked and popped and it began its descent to the forest floor.

Brian stood, one foot propped on the trunk, blowing at the tip of his chainsaw from a safe distance as if he were a cowboy from an old western, the saw's noise reduced to a low rumble.

The forest fell silent. No more screaming, no bird song, not even an insect buzzed. Just utter stillness

"What on earth was that?" The mayor was the first to speak.

"It was the dryad," Ethan whispered.

Brian threw his head back and laughed. He hadn't heard the screaming with his helmet and hearing protection compounded with the noise of his saw.

"It's true." Ethan stalked forward, towards the crowd.

"Aw, come on dude." One of his coworkers shook his head. "You can't be serious."

Ethan's head snapped in his direction, his wild eyes framed with burst capillaries.

"I saw her. I saw her fall and bleed sap. I heard her scream. You all heard her scream."

Brian threw an arm around Ethan's shoulder. "Put away that superstitious bullshit. It was just the whine of the saw echoing, not some crazy tree-hugger."

"I'm telling you, I saw her." Ethan wrenched away

then grabbed for the saw. "We can't do this. We shouldn't be here."

His boss shoved him backwards. "Did you hit your head? Fairytales aren't real, man. Pull it together and do your job."

"No!" Ethan yelled, grabbing for the chainsaw again, and again Brian shoved him back.

Ethan saw red as he hauled back and threw his fist at Brian's face, connecting with the side of his jaw with a wicked right hook.

Brian shoved him away, and he stumbled back a few steps.

"Brady, get off this work site," Brian snarled, his face stony. "Cool off and come back tomorrow, and be ready to do your job. Pull this shit again, and you're gone, got it?"

Ethan growled something under his breath, threw his helmet to the ground, and stalked towards his truck. His wheels kicked up rocks as he sped down the dirt road towards the hotel.

Screeching to a halt in the lot, he parked crookedly between two spaces. He stomped his way into the building, intending to head straight to his room

"Hey there!" the perky receptionist called; her face lit with a smile.

"Not interested," Ethan snapped, stunning her into silence.

The screams reverberated through the entire town, carried by the trees that lined the streets and grew in yards. The glass in the hotel windows rattled with it.

"What the hell is that?" the receptionist gasped, her eyes wide with horror.

Ethan turned to her. "It's the Oak Grove dryad." He stalked towards the stairs to his room. Once inside, he stripped off his sweat-soaked clothes, leaving them in a dirty heap by the bed, and strode naked to the bathroom. Reaching into the shower, he turned on the water as hot as it would go, then stepped under the punishing spray.

In a desperate attempt to drown out the dryad's screams, he covered his ears with his hands and sank to his knees in the shower stall, letting the water sluice over him.

The feeling of her hands on his face and that look in her eyes, right before it all happened, had been enchanting. But now, all he could see was the pain and sheer rage as her trees wrapped themselves around her.

9

Ethan paced around his hotel room with a white towel slung low around his waist while rivulets of now cold water tracked over his bare skin.

I should probably get dressed, he thought, riffling through his bag for something clean. He sniffed a pair of blue Carharrts he was fairly certain he washed before packing and grabbed boxer briefs, socks, and an old warn tee that was moments away from becoming a cleaning rag.

He stared blankly at the clothing laying on the left-hand bed as Feya's screams continued echoing around his skull. Maybe the ringing was permanently scarred there. He sat, leaning over his bent knees and shoving his fingers into his damp hair. He felt as if the dryad's pain was his fault. He was a part of the crew, even if he hadn't made the first cut.

He wondered if there had been any other dryads that he and his coworkers had torn to shreds. Maybe if they slept, they didn't feel it. That would be the best-case scenario. Thinking back over the years, he tried to remember if there had been any other screams blamed on chain saws or equipment in need of care.

This was his job and he had to find a way to make it stop. He shed the towel, tossing it to the floor by the bathroom, then yanked his clothes on. He grabbed his old Hammond Lumber hat and fitted it over his head on his way out the door.

The sun sank as Ethan headed towards the grove. He had to find Feya; had to find out if she was alright. He'd shoved a flashlight in one pocket and a bottle of water in another. She might need some care, but he had no clue what kind of first aid a dryad should receive. Did he treat her as a human? A tree? From what he'd seen, she was a hybrid between the two.

He passed the wrapped statue in the middle of the parking lot and thought the artist had been a bit off on the design. They probably had never seen their subject in person.

The log truck was gone, probably filled with the downed trees they'd thinned from the park area. The enormous feller buncher stood sentinel in front of the woods, a hulking mass wreathed in growing shadows. A camper, probably Brian's, was parked near some convenient RV hook-ups. Years ago, the town had installed RV hookups and a small campground for tourists who wished to stay on-site, rather than in the hotel or near-by bed and breakfast. The light was on inside, and Ethan could hear a TV droning.

Not wanting to be seen, Ethan kept to the shadows. He was good at moving with stealth. His maternal grandfather had been a lover of his land and had taught Ethan and Ethan's father how to travel through it respectfully. His father had loved the land as well as his neighbors. He'd been kind and always went out of way to provide a helping hand to anyone who needed it. It had devastated their whole community when he'd died so suddenly.

The park area was far too quiet. There should have been night birds and insects going about their business, but the damage had been done.

Once he broke through the line of thinned trees to the untouched woods, there was a marked difference in the atmosphere. He could have sworn he was being watched. He'd even stopped a few times to look around him, but nothing made itself known.

The sun sank below the horizon, and the heavy feeling of the air lifted. The nocturnal sounds rose in volume, and he stilled to take it all in, hoping to hear or see some sign of the dryad.

He headed deeper, and something skittered past his ankles. He didn't pay it any mind. It hadn't felt like something that wished him harm.

A silent presence drifted low, and he just made out the immense wingspan of a great horned owl. Its wicked claws had been a whisper above his head. Swooping upward, it alighted on a branch and watched him with moon and starlight glinting off its predatory eyes.

Ethan darted his gaze away out of instinct, then asked, "Do you know where the dryad is?" Worse case, and most likely, it wouldn't understand him.

The owl took to the air.

Ethan dashed forward, trying to keep pace with the nocturnal raptor as it wove its way through the night.

Farther and deeper they moved until the bird glided to the ground, settling next to a body that was far too still.

Breathing hard, Ethan crashed to his knees beside Feya. She was unconscious, but he could see the rise and fall of her chest. Unable to pull on a glamour in such a state, she lay in her true form with all her bark brown skin exposed to the spring air.

Ethan yanked his shirt over his head, and gently pulled her up and against him so he could dress her in it. It barely covered her as he scooped her up in his arms and cradled her close to his chest.

The owl bobbed its head at him, took flight, and led the way once more. Ethan stumbled over roots and underbrush as he struggled to keep the bird in sight. It circled a couple of times, but eventually led them out of the woods in a different area from where he'd entered.

"Thanks!" he called to the owl, still not knowing what it could comprehend.

He had no clue what to do with her. He didn't think calling an ambulance would be wise. They'd have no idea how to treat someone like her.

His mind roved over what he'd seen of the town then recalled Feya mentioning her florist friend. No name came to his mind, but he knew where her shop was. Hopefully she'd know what to do.

He ran towards town, behind the used bookstore, then took a left, praying that he wasn't jostling his precious cargo too much. His only goal was to catch the florist before she closed shop for the night.

He was in luck. A woman was climbing into a dark SUV right outside the building.

TABBY WAS JUST ABOUT to pull out onto Main Street when a figure dashed in front of her. Her headlights illuminated an unfamiliar man cradling a woman in his arms. Stomping on the break, she parked the vehicle, threw the door open, and poked her head over it to see.

"What's going on?" she asked as her eyes took in the man's limp, unconscious burden and the otherworldly look of her.

"Is that Feya?" she gasped, stepping from behind the door.

"It is," the man said. "Are you her florist friend?"

"Yeah, I am. What happened to her?" she rushed forward to check on Feya and beheld the cuts, bruises, and oozing sap. "Oh my god," she whispered.

"Can you help?" he asked, still clutching the dryad tight to his chest.

"I hope so. Get in, we'll take her to my house and see what we can do."

The man didn't say a word as he climbed into the back seat and continued cradling Feya.

Tabby pushed the speed limit even though she didn't live far from the shop. She didn't dare waste any time.

As soon as she put her vehicle into park, she was out her door and opening the back to help the stranger bring her friend into her home.

She fit her key into the lock, flipped on the lights, and led the way to the living room.

"Get her settled on the couch," Tabby directed. "I'll find some towels and water to get her cleaned up, then we'll see."

ETHAN SETTLED Feya gently on the dark blue couch, sank to the floor next to her, and lifted her hand in his, inspecting the injuries criss-crossing over her arm. He slowly worked his way down her body and found the worst damage was to her feet and ankles. Right where the saws would have bit into the trunks of her trees, further cementing the reality of her species.

The woman rushed into the room carrying a bowl of water and a handful of towels. She knelt by Feya's ankles and began dabbing at the wounds with gentle touches.

"I'm Tabby, by the way," she said, working diligently to remove the fluid so she could better assess the damage.

"Ethan." He concentrated as he applied a damp towel to her hands, then up her arms, meticulous with his touch not to disturb any sapped-over wounds. "So, what do you think we should do?"

Tabby sat back on her heels, dropping her towel on the coffee table. "I'm going to treat her as if she's a tree. She's bleeding sap, and from what I can see, the tissue underneath resembles wood."

"Is her skin really bark then?" Ethan asked.

"Yes. Here, have a closer look."

He gently set her hand down then scooted down to where Tabby had been working. Now that the wounds were clean, he could clearly see the bark covering the green wood underneath. The cuts were jagged, and he grimaced at the pain she must have felt.

"So what's your plan, exactly?" he asked.

"I'm going to treat her by scribing away the dead tissue so she can heal properly."

"Scribing?"

"Cutting. You cut away the dead or damaged bark so that the wound is clean and can heal without disease or parasites.

His face blanched at the thought of causing her further pain.

Reading the look on his face as if she'd seen him every day for years, she nodded.

"What should I do?" he asked.

Tabby grimly assessed the situation. "You are going to hold her down."

Tabby left Ethan cleaning around the rest of the minor wounds. She gathered her tools, and washed her hands.

She heard the front door swing open and then her son's voice. "Oh shit!"

She dashed back out to the living room to see her son, standing wide eyed in the middle of the room.

She laid her tools out on the coffee table within easy reach of the couch. "Lucas, why don't you give us a hand, Feya was injured by the logging. This isn't going to be easy."

Ethen remained by Feya's head while Luke took up position by her middle.

"Ready boys?" Tabby asked, palming her grafting knife.

They both nodded grimly and took hold of the unconscious creature.

As soon as Tabby began cutting away the dead tissue, Feya woke with a piercing scream.

Ethan leaned down and spoke softly in her ear. She continued to sob but calmed at his touch.

Within half an hour, the worst was over, and Luke released his hold. "I'm gonna get cleaned up and get supper started, okay Mom?" He wiped his sap drenched hands on his pants.

"That would be great, sweetheart. Thank you."

He kissed his mom's cheek then left the room.

Feya was now sitting up, sobbing on Ethan's bare shoulder. Tabby hadn't even registered that her friend had been wearing a shirt and this man was not. He'd literally given an unconscious woman the shirt off his back.

She touched a hand to his shoulder, then followed her son upstairs. She could hear him rummaging in his room as she knocked on his door.

"Come in!" he called.

She let herself in. "Hey, would you mind if Ethan borrowed a shirt from you? I think he put his on Feya."

"Yeah, sure." He pulled open a dresser drawer, grabbed a black tee shirt with a large Pikachu emblazoned on the front, and held it out to her.

She frowned at her son.

"What? It's clean." He gave it a little shake, making the cartoon do a little dance.

She grabbed the shirt and headed to her own room to gather some clothes for Feya.

Back down stairs, she and Ethan helped Feya pull on a pair of gray lounge pants and a navy sweatshirt.

Ethan accepted the tee-shirt and pulled it on without comment, as if he wore garish cartoon characters on his chest every day.

Tabby inspected Feya's ankles. "They already look better. You heal fast, huh?"

"I do, but I've never taken on damage like this before. Can I have some water?" She tucked her ankles up beside her on the couch.

Tabby stroked her friend's hair then kissed her forehead. "Of course."

IO

abby stood at the sink, rinsing the final pan from
supper. The evening had both flown by, yet
crawled like a snail on snow. Now that Feya was
on the mend, she allowed herself to take a breath.

At the time, she had no idea if her treatment plan
would be correct. She thanked the universe that she'd gone
with her gut.

The front door creaked open and Tim, her boyfriend,
walked into the kitchen. He leaned in and gave her a soft
kiss, then got distracted by the goings on. Soft voices in the
living room invaded their privacy, and Tim noted the
bowls and damp towels littering the counter.

"What's going on?" he laid a gentle hand at the small
of Tabby's back.

Sighing, she leaned back into his comforting warmth.
"We had a little bit of an emergency, but we're good now."

Tim wrapped his arms around her. "Who's in the other
room?"

"Oh, sorry, I forgot you haven't met Feya yet. Give me
a sec, and I'll make introductions." She wiped her hands

and put away the dry dishes, then took Tim's hand and led him to the living room where Feya, Ethan, and Luke sat.

Tim's jaw dropped and he stilled as if frozen at the sight of the fae woman sitting on the couch.

"Tim, this is Feya. She's the Oak Grove Dryad. And that's Ethan. He's working with the company that's supposed to be clear cutting the oaks. And this," she placed an open palm on his chest right over his heart, "is my boyfriend, Tim."

At the mention of cutting, Feya's features hardened and her eyes flashed with barely suppressed rage.

"Sick business, how they set all this up. Pretending that all those meetings were on the books ahead of time." Tim kissed the top of Tabby's head before she slid out from under his arm and took a seat on the recliner.

"Well, you know my opinion on Fred-dick." She settled further into the cushions and popped up the footrest.

"I do. And it's a pleasure to meet you, Ethan," He held his hand out to the other man. "And Feya. You're a dryad?"

The fae flicked her eyes up toward her hair made up of twigs and greenery and smiled. "Last I checked."

Tim seemed to be taking this all rather well. Tabby looked him over, trying to find any sign that he was hiding something. His face remained gentle and kind. This was the man she loved so much. He took everything in stride. She knew he'd think more on it later, perhaps rehash it all with her, but he'd never challenge someone when his eyes backed up their words.

"Ethan, Feya, you're welcome to stay here. I don't have a guest room but there's the couch and this recliner." She patted the arm of the worn chair.

"That's fine," said Ethan, standing. He turned to Feya, who glanced up at him. "I can stay here with you, if you want. Or I can bring you back to the grove…" He dropped off, waiting on Feya's thoughts.

Slowly, she rose off the couch. "I'd like to go with you, if you don't mind." She conjured her own clothes, leaving the set borrowed from Tabby in a neatly folded pile on the coffee table.

"Sure, come on." He offered her his hand, then tucked it around his arm, so she could use him for support if she needed.

MAKING their way through downtown via the sidewalk, Ethan felt the woman clutching his bicep sway. Without missing a beat, he swung her up in his arms.

Her arms snaked around his neck for support. "Oh, you don't have to carry me, I just lost my balance a little."

He held her tighter. "I don't mind if you don't."

She snuggled in, her nose buried between his shoulder and his neck. A thrill at her closeness zipped down Ethan's spine, and he willed himself not to falter. This beautiful, fantastic, enrapturing creature in his arms did things to him he never felt before.

He cleared his throat. "So, how far into the woods do you need to be?"

"Oh, did you not want me to stay with you?" she asked, pulling back a little to look at his face which was shadowed by the dark.

His steps slowed as he absorbed her words. "With me? You mean in my hotel room?"

"Of course." She settled back in, the tip of her nose feathering against his skin.

"Uh, Feya." He gently set her on her feet, his hands

remaining on her waist as he looked down into her wild eyes. "What are you saying?"

"Well, I'm assuming there's a bed in there." She glanced down at his forearms, then back up at his face, her expression solemn yet open.

"Two, actually."

"I think we only need the one." She leaned in close, her hands sliding up his chest, skimming over the muscles she hadn't appreciated while she'd been injured.

"Feya," he whispered, his fingers moving up her back, then playing in the ends of her hair. It wasn't hard and sharp like he'd imagined. The twig-like strands were soft and supple and so alive. He marveled at the feel of it. His forehead came to rest on hers, their lips a breath apart.

She lifted a little on her bare toes and ghosted her lips over his, then reached up to stroke the hair at the nape of his neck.

"You smell nice," she whispered against his mouth.

Ethan held in a groan, then pulled back. "Come on, Feya. Let's keep moving."

"Your room?"

"Yeah, my room." He kept an arm at her waist, but she seemed to be regaining her strength rapidly. It was a couple of miles to the hotel, but it seemed to take only moments to get there.

The receptionist didn't say a word as they made their way into the hotel lobby and then into the elevator. Feya clutched his arms at the elevator's movement and didn't let go until the doors opened.

"I didn't like that method of travel." She scowled at the doors after stepping into the carpeted hall.

"Me either, I just thought it would be better than the stairs. Come on." He grabbed her hand and gave her a little tug.

Pulling the key card out of his wallet, he swiped it by the lock and let Feya in.

He shoved his hands in his pockets and watched Feya survey the room as the door clicked shut behind him. She wandered into the bathroom then out into the bedroom area. She tilted her head, studying the beds: one with his bag laying open on it, the other with its rumpled sheets where he'd slept fitfully the night before.

She glided over the rug and tugged the curtains over the windows, before turning to face him.

Her eyes locked on his, soft and steady, and she reached for the hem of her sweatshirt.

His breath caught as she slowly slid the material up her torso, revealing her sensual body. Her fae form was still that of a woman, and his heart beat faster as the fabric slid up over her breasts, then over her head, and snapped from existence before they hit floor. She untied the pants at her waist, and gave a little wriggle so they dropped to her ankles and stepped out of them, leaving her bare before him. The scratches and wounds were now light scars against her dark skin.

She stepped forward until she stood just a breath away from him.

His gaze caught on those scars. Scars his people had given her. He hadn't held the saw, but he was one of them just the same. "I'm so sorry." He held his hands clenched at his sides, feeling unworthy to reach out to her.

"Do you want to touch me, Ethan?" She tilted her head so she could look him in the eyes.

Even if he had wanted to lie, his body would have betrayed him. His heart beat a rapid staccato and his breath came in a heavy puff.

"Yes," he whispered as liquid heat spread through his veins.

She slid her palm up his body and then back down before slipping her hands up under the Pikachu shirt. "Good, because I want to touch you too. Would you like that?"

He nodded, then threaded his fingers into her hair and brought his mouth down on hers. The kiss was feverish, a momentary dance of lips and tongues before Feya pulled back.

"This is not your fault." She ran a fingertip over her skin, bumping over the ridged flesh. "They did not listen and that's on them."

She tipped up on her toes and kissed him again, letting her hands explore, but soon became frustrated with the barrier of clothing.

"I also want to see you." She pulled up on his shirt and helped him out of it. She grabbed the waistband of his jeans and slowly walked backwards, leading him until the back of her legs hit the rumpled bed.

She popped the button, and lowered the zipper, lifting her eyes to his. "Yes?"

"Yes, god, yes." The pitch of his voice dropped with desire.

She licked her lips, sliding to her knees and pulling his pants down his legs, then tugged at the band of his boxer briefs. His erection sprang free, coming to attention right at her level. Touching it with only her tongue, she licked him from base to tip as she removed what remained of his clothes. She sucked him into her mouth, taking him in as far as she could. His shaft was thick and long, so she gripped the base with one hand, while cupping his balls with the other, rolling them with her fingers.

"Holy shit," he whispered, his hands going to her hair.

She sucked him in again, and his hips bucked.

Feya giggled, giving him a few more strokes before

slowly sliding her way up his torso, licking and kissing as she moved. His cock twitched as it slid between her breasts and down her abdomen. Wrapping her legs around him, she tugged him onto the bed with her.

His restraint was wearing thin, so he grabbed her by the waist and heaved her further up on the mattress, then leaned down so his nose grazed the crease at the top of her thigh. She smelled of fresh night air, reminding him yet again that Feya was not human. He slid his tongue through her most sensitive area, flicking over her clit then sucking it lightly.

She gasped and arched her back. He toyed with her just as she'd done to him, before sliding his body up hers, drawing a peaked nipple into his mouth and lavishing it with his tongue.

Feya gasped and her hips rose up to grind on whatever part of him she could reach.

"Good?" he rasped, rolling her nipple with his fingers and taking the other into his mouth.

"Yes," she gasped, again grinding herself against him, making desperate little whimpers.

He slid further up her body, until his thickness found her warmth, and ground against her.

"Should I grab a condom?" he asked, reaching down to tease her opening with his finger, then pushed it inside.

She shook her head. "It isn't my time to reproduce, and I carry no disease. Neither do you. I can smell your health." She nipped at his neck and he groaned again.

His cock throbbed, but he continued exploring her with his fingers.

"Ethan," she whimpered, clinging to him.

"Hm?" he withdrew and pushed another finger inside her along with the first.

"If you aren't inside me in 2 seconds, I'm going to lose my mind."

She reached for him and pumped her hand up his hard length then guided him to her entrance.

Without a word, she thrust upwards, twisting her hips until he was completely seated inside her. They both gasped.

"Fuck, you feel good." Ethan withdrew and thrust into her again. "So, so good."

She thrust up to meet him, then pushed her body up so she was seated on him and ground her center against his pelvis.

She raised herself and then slid back down on him in a sensuous torture. Their bodies writhed together as they chased each other to bliss. She could feel her magic flowing through her and reaching out to him. Her breath caught as something inside him answered, reaching out and twining with her power like a cat rubbing up against a favored individual.

When Feya cried out with her release, she rocked harder, and Ethan soon followed. Sated, they flopped to the bed together, arms and legs entwined.

Feya traced the shell of Ethan's ear then scooted up to lick it.

Ethan groaned and pulled her closer. "I never thought… uh, that was—"

"What happens when two fae find themselves in bed together," Feya supplied.

He pulled back so he could try to read her face; the gentle smile on her lips. "Come again?"

"Oh, I'd love to." She gave him a cheeky grin.

"Feya."

"Ethan. The magic in my blood calls to the magic in yours. Anyway, were you a changeling? Adopted?"

He raised his eyebrows. "I'm confused."

She kissed his nose. "Clearly. You're fae. These ears." She stroked the tip of it which was ever so slightly pointed. "They've been glamoured but they're definitely elf ears."

"Elf. Ears?"

"Of course. Oh! Oh… you didn't know?"

He buried his face in her breasts and groaned again, this time out of frustration, though it was hard to remain that way with her scent filling his nostrils. "I had no idea."

"That's why I'm thinking changeling." She kissed the top of his head. "Your mother might not have even known. Or perhaps her memory was altered."

"The fae can do that?"

"Mm. Some." She slid down, and rested her head on his bicep. "And by the way, you are exceptionally beautiful. Thought you should know."

Ethan blushed then took her mouth with his own and lost himself once more in her embrace. For the moment, he didn't need to think about what he'd just learned.

II

Tabitha and Timothy talked late into the night about myths, the local legend, and what was going on in their community. She gave him every bit of information she had on Feya and he patiently listened. Tim loved Tabby, so her cause became his.

"We'll get some voices on her side, you'll see," he said. "There are plenty of good people here that Alcroft has been trying to work around."

Tabby sighed and snuggled deeper into Tim's comforting embrace. "I hope so. Things haven't been looking so great for Feya. What an awful way to wake up."

A yawn cracked her mouth wide open, and he drew her tighter into his arms, kissing the top of her head. "Sleep. Your worries can wait until tomorrow."

TABBY ROSE EARLY and headed out after completing her morning routine. She'd sent out a mass text to anyone she thought would listen to meet up at The Sip Down.

Unsurprisingly, she was the first one there besides Bill.

She took a seat and pulled out her laptop to aid her, and came up with a game plan about what she was going to say to her friends.

It was out of the question to talk about Feya at this point. She'd left a message on Ethan's phone but hadn't heard back yet. Without the dryad present, there was no way to prove what she was. Instead, she decided to focus on local history and culture.

"Mornin', Tabby Cat," Bill greeted her with the affectionate nickname he'd come up with when she was 3 and he was 9 as he approached her table.

"Hey Bill!" she pushed her chair back and stood, giving him a hug.

They each took a seat to relax for a moment before the day really got going.

"So what's this meeting all about anyhow?" Bill leaned forward, clasping his hands and tapping his thumbs together.

"It's about what Alcroft's been up to."

"That sneaky old bastard. He's been scheduling those town meetings just right, hasn't he."

Tabby nodded. "Exactly. So I want to discuss what we're going to do about it."

Bill stood. "Sounds good to me. Can I get you anything?"

"A black coffee would be fantastic."

"You got it!" He patted her shoulder then headed behind the counter to help his young employee get through the first part of the morning rush.

The door opened, letting in Bev and her husband, John.

"Hey there big sis and John!" Bill called as he bustled around behind the counter.

The couple waved then took a seat at Tabby's table.

A few more neighbors entered, grabbed their coffees to go, while others gathered around Tabby.

When things slowed up a bit, Bill rejoined the group.

"Okay." Tabby stood and angled her laptop so everyone could see the split screen of a map of the town and her notes. "Okay. So as you know, Alcroft has been very selective with the timing of his town meetings lately." She launched into her issues with what he was doing then ended with, "Not only is he destroying something that tourists come from out of state to visit, he's also tearing down a natural phenomena. I can't find anything about any other groves around here that are only oaks that weren't deliberately planted or cultivated that way."

"How do we know our grove wasn't?" a woman with short dark hair asked, sounding genuinely curious.

"I've been digging through old town records, and everything I've found says the grove was here long before this area was settled. And as far as I found, this town was settled pre-1700's, possibly around the time of the puritans."

"Well, we always have been a rebellious bunch," Bill joked.

"Yeah well, it's time to bring that rebellion back in order to preserve the very thing this town was named for. We can't be Oak Grove without a grove of oaks." Tabby took a deep breath. "Then the question is, what are we going to do about it?"

Her words hung in the air as her friends and neighbors contemplated the best course of action.

"I know for a fact that the Smiths would be more than happy to sell off some acreage for development. They're getting older and none of their kids live around here anymore and none of them have any interest in coming back and to take over the farm." Rachelle, the local Methodist minister, pointed out the plot of land on the map pulled up on Tabby's screen. "It's even a better location. It doesn't need near the amount of work to clear, and the oaks that are growing there would be easy to build around, which would keep up with the town's image. It's closer to the school too, so kids could play there. I've heard that a park and playground is something they want to build."

"Oh! That's perfect!" Tabby marked down the idea and the reasons why it was a better choice for the town.

A few other points were discussed, but the Smith's land was the best choice by far.

"Now, does anyone have the inside scoop for the next town meeting? I've been looking around downtown and can't find anything," Bev asked before drinking a few mouthfuls of her iced coffee.

The door opened, carrying a breeze that smelled of fresh vegetation. Feya and Ethan walk through, hand in hand. She was wearing her human glamour once more, signaling to Tabby that she must be feeling a heck of a lot better after her ordeal the day before.

Murmurs rose up throughout the little crowd. Some recognized her from her outburst at the last town meeting and knew nothing about her except she came off as a nut job.

Tabby's eyebrows inched up her forehead as she noted the increased closeness between the two newcomers.

"Come on over!" she called, making room for them to pull chairs up. "Feya, Ethan, we were just discussing alternative areas for development."

Feya's face lit up.

"Really? That's wonderful!" She plopped herself down

on Tabby's left, and leaned over to read the notes her friend put together.

Ethan leaned down and kissed the top of Feya's head before approaching the front counter to get them drinks and breakfast.

"Everyone, this is Feya." Tabby set a gentle hand on the youthful woman's shoulder. "She has deep roots in this town and is as passionate about this subject, if not more so, than any of us."

Tabby leaned over to whisper in Feya's ear, "I haven't told them anything about you being a dryad yet. Figured it was best to use history and tourism as a platform."

Feya nodded and gave a little wave to the gathering. "Mind if I say a few words?"

Tabby gestured around, "Go right on ahead."

"Yes, hi. I'm Feya, and I do have very, very deep roots here in Oak Grove. The grove this town was named for has lived in harmony with this town for hundreds of years. I'm sure you've heard the stories. I won't go into detail about any truth behind them but just know there is some. The grove has never been cut. Not even the saplings which were planted by the original settlers. Have you ever wondered why that is? Why you don't find acorns underfoot beneath your trees, why the squirrels and chipmunks that harvest them don't hide their stashes in the ground on your land like they do in the grove. I'd say with no uncertainty that the agreement holds historical fact."

Feya accepted a cup of herbal tea from Ethan and warmed her hands around it.

"Oh, that's fascinating!" Tabby said, stalling any attendees from dismissing Feya's words. "I hadn't thought about that. It's fascinating how nature seems to prove the legend, isn't it?"

"Aren't you the girl who freaked out at the last town meeting?" a gentleman that Tabby didn't recognize asked.

Feya simply shrugged then nodded. "Yes. As it's been mentioned, this is very important to me."

The discussion moved on to more mundane topics and the group dispersed leaving Tabby, Tim, Bev, Bill, Rachelle, Feya, and Ethan to a more intimate conversation.

Rachelle studied Feya with a frown. The dryad shifted in her seat, uncomfortable with the scrutiny.

The minister shook her head. "I'm sorry. I didn't mean to stare so hard at you. I just recognize you from somewhere and I can't for the life of me put my finger on where."

Tabby bit her lip and glanced at Feya, who shrugged, then back at Rachelle.

"Well, there's a portrait of her at the historical society. A pen and ink." Tabby drummed her fingers on the table, not knowing how much she should reveal.

"Actually, that artist did a number of drawings. I bet one made it over to the church. He also made those stained glass windows," said Feya.

"Oh! That's it!" Rachelle snapped her fingers. "There's a pen and ink in the basement. You're the spitting image of the original model. You weren't kidding when you said you have deep roots here. That's some strong genetics."

"He was a talented artist." Feya glanced at Tabby, trusting her friend to gauge who was safe to reveal the truth to. She'd been welcome in the church in the past, but years could change things.

Tabby sighed. "Rachelle, Feya *is* the original model."

All eyes turned to Feya, some in confusion, some already in the know.

"I don't understand," said Rachelle, her eyebrows drawing in confusion.

Feya glanced to the front of the cafe and noted that no one else was present. Even the girl who was running the front counter was currently out back.

"I'm the dryad of Oak Grove. The grove is my home and has been for several hundred years."

Rachelle made a strangled sound then spluttered into her coffee.

"I can show you if you want," Feya offered, standing.

"I don't think we need to go traipsing around town so you can vanish into a tree," Tabby muttered.

"I wasn't going to. I was just going to drop my glamour." Feya giggled. She'd learned a lot over the past few days, including how best to prove herself.

Tabby's cheeks flushed. "Oh."

Feya laughed again and dropped her glamour for a few seconds so Rachelle and the others could see her true form.

"Oh! Oh my!" The older woman thumped her chest with her open palm. "You weren't kidding! Well, I believe there's a lot of mystery left to this world. Stands to reason there'd be a few around here!"

"You have no idea," Feya muttered, casting her eyes at Ethan, who frowned at her. He wasn't ready to talk about what he might be yet. He needed to come to grips with it himself first.

12

"So you two are a thing now?" Tabby asked Feya. They sat in her kitchen, pouring over the notes taken and the marks on the map printed out from the meeting.

Feya blushed. "Yes. It's been a very long time since I've been with a male like this. He's like me." She paused and lowered her voice. "Don't bring it up though. He just found out and he's still in a bit of shock over it."

"What do you mean he's like you? He's a dryad?" Tabby's eyebrows knit together in confusion.

"Oh, no. I mean he's fae, an elf actually. At first, I thought maybe he was a changeling, but now I think maybe there's more to it than that. I wish I could speak to his family, but that's currently out of the question. Everyone remembers his father as a wonderful, kind, helpful man. I suspect he was or maybe even still is and he put those memories in people's heads before he had to leave. I think that maybe the local tribes have fae roots. I mean, those I've met before now have been human, but Ethan definitely is not. An elf sire could have overwhelmed his essence as he developed, especially if there was an answering essence in the mother."

"Huh." Tabby nodded slowly. "That's quite interesting actually."

"Perhaps. More people had fae in them throughout history than you know. They were once as common a people in this world as humans and often intermarried. I bet there's many that have more than a drop of fae essence in their blood now." Feya tapped the map, finding it hard to look away from the plot of land that was her grove. "Not the mayor though."

Tabby snorted and began sorting the papers into piles. "I wouldn't think so. He's pretty much a purebred jackass."

Feya barked out a laugh. "There are plenty of fae assholes, but I can't disagree with you even a little." She'd started using more modern lingo in her speech and liked how it rolled off her tongue.

"So tell me about Tim." Feya abruptly changed the topic. "How did you two meet? He seems like a good man."

Tabby's smile softened. "He's a very good man. Our history is a little complicated though."

Feya sat back and crossed her arms. "I've got time."

"All right," said Tabby. "Well, he was my ex-husband's friend. One of his closest. He's one of those quiet hard-working types. Tim, not my ex." She cracked a smile. "Anyway. He's always been around, and was always willing to help the sperm-donor—I mean my husband out. After Lucas was born, he got busier at work, which turned out to be code for sleeping with Tim's wife."

Feya's eyes widened. "No way. This sounds like one of those novels you have on the top of your bookshelf!"

"What were you doing snooping on the top of my bookshelf?" Tabby pinched her lip between her teeth and scowled, but couldn't hold it for long, before rolling her eyes. "You're not wrong. Anyways, this went on for years while the two of them used Tim and I as alibies. Anyway, when Lucas was 7, the shit hit the fan."

"That sounds messy," said Feya, eyebrows raising.

"It's a metaphor. Well anyhow, Tim caught them. He went through a messy divorce. Mine was less messy. My husband just signed the papers and left. We haven't heard from him since, not even a birthday card to his son, no contest over assets, just up and left and never looked back."

"So how long before you and Tim became lovers?" Feya jumped straight to the point.

"It was a while. I was bitter and adjusting to raising my son on my own. It was actually Lucas who bonded with Tim first. He was having trouble at school, and I was at a loss. Well since Tim only lives a few houses down, he heard one of our shouting matches one night and heard Luke storm out. When he walked by Tim's house, Tim asked for his help with some yard work."

"Which was code for teaching him how to be a man?" asked Feya.

"Essentially yes," said Tabby. "They spent more and more time together, then one night, Luke asked to invite Tim to dinner. We ended up talking for hours, then we went out for coffee, then dinner, which eventually turned into us falling in love."

"I'm glad he's been so good to you and Luke. Someone like that is someone worth holding onto. Now tell me, how is the sex?" Feya's eyes gleamed with mischief.

Tabby sat straight with mock horror, her finger tips flying to her chest over her heart. "That is none of your business. But it's good. Very good."

Tabby's phone rang in her pocket, and Feya jumped at the sudden noise.

"Hey, Bill." Tabby excused herself from the room.

Feya went to the fridge and helped herself to some carrots while she waited for her friend to return.

Her thoughts wandered to the night before, and a smile lifted her lips. It had indeed been a very long time since she'd been touched and had touched someone in return. She'd felt more alive in Ethan's arms than she had in hundreds of years. What's more, the fae in him called to the same in her, and they connected on an extraordinarily deep level. She'd never been intimate with one of her kind before, to her knowledge. She couldn't remember her mother; never-mind any familial bond they may have had.

Feya had started out like most other dryads: as something else. In her case, she had been an elf. She'd been cursed into a tree by one of the old gods. Well, it had felt like a curse. Over the years, she'd grown to love what she was and what she could do. But now that she'd found Ethan, she missed being someone who could move about the world.

Tabby reentered the kitchen and deposited her phone on the counter. "I'm sure you heard, but that was Bill. He overheard a customer talking about a town meeting. Tonight. Are you ready to try again?"

Feya nodded. "As I'll ever be."

ETHAN RETURNED to work wearing his hardhat, chaps, and steel toed boots, but he had no intention of doing any actual cutting. He didn't know what he was going to say to Brian. He wouldn't apologize for his behavior.

He needn't have worried. When he arrived at the job site, Brian had informed him that he was temporarily demoted to gopher and was stuck doing paperwork, which he could do from his hotel room.

He was happy to note that the rest of the logging team wasn't cutting. With a town meeting tonight, it was decided that the crew should hold off and focus on clean-up instead. The thinning had been intended to make the area more aesthetically pleasing to tourists, so it was their job to not just cut trees, but also to haul away the brush and smooth the ground. It wasn't their normal work, not to this extent, but the town of Oak Grove was paying them well.

He hopped into his truck and headed back to his hotel room. He'd only been on his laptop for 20 minutes when a knock at the door interrupted him.

He stood and stretched before padding to the door to squint through the peephole.

Feya stood in the hall, raising her knuckles to knock again. Before they could connect, he opened the door and lifted her into his arms.

She squealed and clutched his shoulders as he bent his head and smothered his face in her belly.

Kicking the door shut, he carried her over to the bed and fell onto it with her.

"I had a feeling you'd be here," she whispered, then gasped as he gently bit her breast through her shirt. "Oh, gods yes. Glad we agree." She ground her body as close to his as she could and reveled in the feel of him against her.

"Mmph," he said, his face still buried against her.

She wriggled so she could get her hands under his shirt, scratching and exploring his skin with her finger tips. The smell that came off him was pure magic. Whether he knew what he was or not, he'd used his magic before. Being a logger, she suspected a lot of his powers had gone into healing the land after he'd taken from it.

He pulled up on her shirt, yanking it up over her head.

She didn't wear a bra. She couldn't get used to the feeling of one, so he was happy to be greeted by her peeked nipples, he latched his lips around one and swirled his tongue over the raised bud.

Feya gasped at the feeling of his wet mouth on her, arching her back to demand more. He greedily complied, lavishing her other breast with attention while he rolled her damp nipple between his fingers.

She wriggled some more, pushing his shirt up farther, until he had to separate his mouth from her skin so she could remove the material. Her hands moved down to his jeans, undoing them and shoving them down his legs.

His erection strained against his black boxer briefs, and she soon had him freed from those as well. Grabbing his shaft, she gave it a few firm pumps before removing her own pants and climbing on top of him.

Her breasts swung over his face, and he was more than happy to give them his undivided attention as she rode him to their mutual bliss. After they both finished shuddering, they twisted in the bed so they could lay facing each other, Feya's leg thrown over his waist, keeping him inside her for as long as possible, while a current of magic zinged through their veins.

This was something she hadn't known she'd been missing. She'd thought she was in love with that artist all those years ago. Maybe she had been, after a fashion, but the way her essence called to Ethan's was something completely different, like her soul had found a piece she'd never known she was missing, claiming him as hers.

She saw a clarity come to his eyes as he reached for her face, stroking her cheeks with his thumbs.

"Something just happened, didn't it?" he whispered, touching his forehead to hers.

"Something wonderful." She smiled and tilted her

head so she could kiss him. "Before I was a dryad, I was an elf too. Your essence calls to mine."

"Is it like a fated-mates thing?" his hand slid from her face, down her arm, and came to rest on her hip.

"Not exactly. In the fae world, mates aren't fated like in all the books humans love. They're chosen. When every fiber of your being connects with another, including your heart, we call them mates."

"Does that mean you want this as much as I do?" his hand slid around to grab her ass, and pull her closer to him. His cock began hardening again inside her.

"Maybe even more." Her words came out in a pant.

"It's only been a few days." He rocked his hips, sinking deeper.

Her leg tightened around him, encouraging his movements. "When you know, you know. I've never been more certain in my life. Insta-love though it may be." She pulled out a phrase she'd found online for characters in romance stories that fell in love right away.

He rolled her underneath him and his thrusts became more urgent. "Love, uh?" He lowered his head and kissed her again.

"Yes." She growled, thrusting her hips up to meet his, and wrapping her other leg around him.

When they were both satisfied, he reluctantly pulled out of her warmth and tucked her close to his body, pulling the covers over them both.

"I love you too," he whispered.

She smiled and sighed happily.

As the sun sank, the people of Oak Grove gathered in the town hall. The crowd was bigger than the last as the word spread to those Mayor Alcroft hoped to avoid.

The core group of Feya's team had met for supper beforehand, so they could arrive together as a unified front.

Ethan, though not a resident of Oak Grove, attended as moral support for his mate. *His mate.* He loved the idea of that. He kissed her temple and tucked her hair behind her ear.

The mayor called the meeting to order, glaring out over the gathering. He didn't appreciate being out-maneuvered. He promised himself he'd find out who had the big mouth and would deal with them later.

The florist, the pastor, the bartender—all the thorns in his side, including the crazy girl—were present.

He opened the meeting, bringing up general business for a few minutes before buckling down to the main topic of the meeting.

"The progress on the grove is going well. The loggers have cleared most of the brush from the tourist area and are now ready to start clear cutting the rest. Very soon, we'll have a beautiful park and so much more."

Tabby stood, taking a deep breath, and waited to be acknowledged.

"Yes, Ms. Richards. Go ahead." He motioned for her to speak.

Tabby launched into their group's idea for an alternate location for the development and all the benefits the Smith's fields would supply, including cutting costs on logging.

Frederick shook his head. "I'm afraid the wheels are already in motion, Tabitha. This is the course of action we decided to pursue."

Tim stood, and put his arm around her shoulders.

"Those actions weren't agreed on by everyone. You held meetings without announcing them in order to sway the vote your way."

"That's utterly ridiculous, Timothy."

"Is it?" Rachelle stood next. "I don't recall being informed, and I help run the town's website. Can you explain that oversight?"

Fredrick smiled at the minister. "It was just that, an oversight. They happen from time to time. We are only human, after all."

"Speak for yourself." Feya stood next.

"Young lady, you were asked to remove yourself from these meetings. Please step outside."

"No. I wasn't banned from all meetings, and I have things that need to be said." She stood on her seat so the crowd could better see and hear her. "We spoke with the Smiths. They would be more than happy to sell their land to the town. Grateful, in fact. The grove was never meant to be touched by ax or saw."

"It's trees, young lady. They don't have feelings," he interrupted her.

Her anger grew and her voice turned cold. "That's where you're wrong. Those trees are a part of me, and I most definitely have feelings on this."

Alcroft sneered at her. "Really, miss—"

"My name is Feya."

"Of course, Feya." His voice turned indulgent, as if speaking to a small child.

"You had to have heard her screams when those trees came down the other day." Ethan found he couldn't stay silent any longer. "Every cut left wounds on her. She felt every tree as they fell."

"She looks fine to me." Fredrick's face hardened. His mask of congenial gentlemen disintegrated.

"As I said before, not all of us are human." Feya dropped her glamour like a garment. One moment she looked as human as everyone else, the next she was the beautiful creature of the woods.

The crowd gasped, but the mayor began laughing.

"I don't know what this is, but you are far too late. The decision is made."

Ethan could feel the rage building under Feya's skin, and he looked to Tabby with fear in his eyes. He had no idea what she was capable of, but he did know that this wasn't a good place to unleash.

The two of them managed to usher her out the door amidst rising tempers and voices.

The rage rolled off her in terrible waves as they stood on the sidewalk.

"I will end them," Feya hissed, her fists clenching and unclenching. "I will destroy them if they continue with this."

"Feya—" Ethan reached out to her.

"No!" she shrieked, not wanting comfort. None of this was okay, and his body couldn't sooth what was now flowing through her veins. "This will not stand." She stalked down the road to the first available oak tree and disappeared.

13

The rumble of log trucks drew the attention of the Oak Grove residents going about their morning.

The first crested the hill; a behemoth of a machine hauling an empty trailer. The rumble grew louder as it approached and people stopped to watch it pass. The second crested a moment later. They made it through the downtown area and turned down the narrow drive that led to Oak Park.

Ethan rested his hand on the side of the bed Feya had occupied for several evenings. He hadn't seen her since she'd taken off during the town meeting. It had been too dark to even think about hunting her in the woods, but with the sun risen he had to find her. He knew this was the day that the clear cutting began. He couldn't think of anything he could do to stop it, but he wanted to be with her when it happened; wanted to hold her as her screams ripped through the forest. He wished he could absorb her pain into himself, but her trees were entangled in her DNA.

Dressing and throwing a baseball cap over his dark hair, he headed out. He climbed into his truck and drove past the park entrance until he arrived at the Methodist church. The grove extended out behind it, so it was there he intended to begin his search.

His was the only vehicle in the lot, but he still locked his doors, pocketing the keys. He hitched his backpack filled with water bottles, snacks, and bandages up on his shoulders. He didn't know what good the food would do, but Feya would definitely need water.

The field behind the church grew in an untamed, dense growth of wildflowers, clover, and grass. The morning dew clung to his boots and dampened the bottom of his jeans.

In the distance, the rumble of machinery warned him there wasn't much time. Ethan picked up his pace, running to the tree line, then jogged through the oaks. He couldn't sprint like he wanted to. He needed to be able to listen and pay the utmost attention to his surroundings.

There was no telling where Feya might be. She could be inside any of the hundreds of trees, or she could be heading towards the crew to fight for her home. Or she could be waiting in there, not that she knew he was coming to her but just communing with her trees.

A flock of chickadees darted into his path, dive-bombing him and chicka-deeing on top of their little voices, their movements frantic.

"Do you know where Feya is?" he asked.

Deeeeeeee! shrieked one, flapping its little wings for all it was worth.

Ethan picked up his pace, trying to keep up with their jagged flightpath. The deeper they led him, the more he recognized his surroundings. The closer to the center of the grove, the bigger and older the trees grew until he finally entered a small clearing dominated by the biggest oaks of all.

Feya sat on the ground, hugging her knees. She looked up as she heard his footsteps, then jumped to her feet.

"Ethan. Oh, Ethan. I'm sorry I ran away last night. I just don't know what to do. They won't stop!" Tears leaked down Feya's cheeks and dripped from her chin.

"Sweetheart." Ethan gathered her in his arms and tucked her head under his chin. "You don't need to be sorry. I can't imagine what this is doing to you. I don't know what to do either, but I do know I want to be here for you. As little good as that does."

She sobbed softly into his shoulder, and he stroked her back.

"This does a lot of good." She sniffled and wiped at her face with the back of her hand. "I wish I'd known to let you get close the last time. I don't want to be alone."

The dull sound of machinery filtered through the trees, and Feya abruptly tensed.

"Don't let go of me." She clung to Ethan, her fingers digging into his skin.

He tightened his arms around her. "Never."

She whimpered as she clung, and Ethan felt her react to the first cut. He held her tight as her legs gave way, and he sank to the ground with her, pulling her onto his lap and wrapping his body around her as completely as he could.

Sap flowed from her mangled ankles and she shuddered as the tree fell, her keening momentarily deafening Ethan.

He continued holding her to him, offering as much comfort and support as he could. With one hand, he grabbed two water bottles from his pack. He cracked one open and held it to her lips. Not all of it went in, but she did manage to swallow a little. The other he opened and poured over her healing flesh, keeping it clean as possible.

"Thank you," she whispered just before her body tensed as her legs etched with fresh wounds. His ears rang with her next scream, as if it had been torn up from her toes and punched into his eardrums.

They repeated the process: clinging to one another, a sip of water, a cleansing of the wounds.

Though the trees still shook with it, Feya's cries became hoarse.

Between cuts, Ethan bandaged what he could, then removed his shirt, and wrapped it around her legs in an effort to keep them as clean as possible. Another cut came, and Feya's back arched. Ethan held her through it then peeled the shirt back and dabbed at the wounds with the damp material.

As she screamed again, the trees around them groaned and popped. The branches moved, reaching to Feya.

At the next, the ground quaked and something moved underneath them. Ethan was thrust away from the dryad as a large root exploded from the ground, sending dirt and forest debris flying into the air.

"No," Feya whispered, "Don't take him away from me."

The root stilled then slowly slithered backwards into the hole it had created. The branches still reached forward, but instead of pushing Ethan away like the last time, they created a cocoon around them both.

Feya's back arched once more, and Ethan heard a snap. Under his hands, one of her ribs shifted.

"Shit. Feya, I don't know what to do. What do I do?" He didn't want to hurt her further, so he loosened his arms.

She clutched harder at him. "You promised not to go."

"I know. I won't. I just don't want to cause you more pain."

She looked up with him, sap leaking from her eyes, nose, and ears. "What more pain could you cause? Please, I feel like you're the only thing holding me together." She reached up and stroked his face with trembling fingers sticky with sap.

As her body shook, he tightened his arms around her once more. As her body contorted with the next felled tree, he held her tighter still. The bones under his fingers shifted and popped. At one point he felt the bones in her arms splinter, the shards poking through her skin and into his hands.

As much as he wanted to, he couldn't clean her up now, couldn't prevent the damage. She began healing under his fingers, and he clenched his hands firmly around her arm, keeping it straight so it might heal properly.

The next came, and a bone popped through the skin of her thigh, stabbing into his side. He gasped at the impact and sudden pain but didn't pull away. Whatever he had to give, he would give to the woman he loved.

Sap and blood mixed, and the bone retreated inside her leg, the wound sealing behind it.

Feya was too far gone to notice the damage she'd caused. She clung to him with a desperation so strong, it nearly broke him.

Ethan rubbed her back and whispered in her ear that he was there, that he would never leave her.

The oak branches around them blotted out the sky, leaving them in a muffled stillness.

Feya gasped and sat up, taking great gulps of air, then looked down where the blood seeped from Ethan's side.

Cuts appeared on her legs, but lesser than before, and

she was able to manage the pain. The trees around her seemed to be absorbing much of the effects of the cutting.

Ethan slumped, grasping her arms and letting his forehead drop to her shoulder.

"Oh gods," Feya whispered, her hand hovering over the wound her own broken bones had created. "Oh gods."

"It's okay. I'll be okay." Ethan's words came out far more strained than intended.

More shallow slashes appeared on Feya's skin and the sap flowed once more. She looked from her blood to Ethan's and back again. With delicate fingers, she swiped at the sap until her hands were coated in it, then lifted them to the puncture in Ethan's side. Ever so gently, she applied her lifeblood to his wounds.

She gasped as more cuts appeared on her skin, and again she dipped her fingers in it and applied it to Ethan's skin. The sap and blood mixed, and the hole clotted, sealing the wound and holding in the blood that still wanted to flow.

She winced as she took the water soaked rag from her skin, and ripped it into strips, binding Ethan's side with it.

Ethan watched her work and felt her essence mixing with his, felt his body respond and begin healing. So slowly, compared to the dryad, but still much quicker than a human. He could feel the clot tug at his skin as it hardened into a scab; could feel his injuries knitting back together.

Feya uncapped another water bottle and handed it to him. After he finished drinking, she crawled back into his lap, shuddering again and again as her trees were destroyed. Those protecting her also felt the agony of their offspring. And it seemed to Ethan as if he'd become a part of this living organism. That whatever fae magic had slept dormant in his blood all these years had suddenly come to life.

Evening fell and the trees straightened, leaving Feya and Ethan clinging to one another in the open air. The loggers had left the site for the night.

Ethan lifted Feya, and her arms slid around his neck. He thought about bringing her to Tabby again, but he'd already done all that he could to help her. Now, he just wanted to take care of her.

As they emerged from the woods and headed towards the church parking lot, a figure dashed out of a door and ran for them.

Rachelle, gray hair streaming wildly behind her, stopped before them. "Oh, the poor dear!" She gasped at Feya's state. Then her gaze caught on Ethan's bare chest and the strips of fabric bound around him. "What happened?"

Ethan shook his head. "I'm fine. I just want to get Feya to bed so she can rest."

"Okay," said Rachelle, reaching out and stroking the semiconscious creature's hair. "I've been praying all day. It's all I knew to do. I heard the screaming, and knew who it was this time. I prayed and I prayed."

"We appreciate it, thank you." Ethan pressed a button on his key fob, and with a quiet beep, the doors of his truck unlocked.

Feya lifted her head from Ethan and smiled at Rachelle. "I think your prayers were heard. Ethan was with me all day long and the trees accepted him as mine. We took care of each other."

"As it should be." Rachelle reached out with both hands, cupping a cheek of each. "You belong to each other now. No ceremony could tell you that more than what you've experienced together. You take care. Rest. Tomorrow—" Rachelle hesitated. "Tomorrow, it begins again. I pray you survive this." She looked deep into Feya's eyes. "I hope to survive it too."

Feya took the woman's hand in her own. "I swear to you, you will."

14

E than chose to take the stairs to his room this time, Feya still cradled in his arms. She wore only an old blanket he kept in his truck for emergencies as she was too exhausted to glamour clothes.

Once in his suite, he headed straight to the shower and turned the knobs to start the water. He set her gently down on the bathroom's tiled floor, then stripped out of his remaining clothes.

Hissing a little, he pulled the makeshift bandage from his wound. Feya pulled herself up onto her knees and kissed the skin next to it.

"It's actually healing nicely. Quickly too," she murmured, feeling the skin around it for excess heat or swelling with gentle touches.

"Thanks to whatever it is you did." Ethan stuck his hand under the running water to gauge the temperature. Warmth licked at his fingertips, so he flipped on the showerhead before lifting Feya into the stall and climbing in with her.

She didn't make a sound as the water hit her wounds,

washing away sap and blood and leaving angry scars behind.

Ethan grabbed a clean washcloth and a bar of soap then lathered her skin with as much care as he could manage. "You're healing well too."

"And that is thanks to you. You being there made all the difference." Her fingers drifted up his torso, coming to rest on his racing heart.

After he finished bathing her, she took the cloth and returned the favor. She watched in appreciation as the bubbles slid over his wet body.

Again, she went to her knees, wiping a spot clean on his upper thigh, then placing a feather-light kiss there. As she pulled back, she washed another spot, and kissed there too.

"Feya," Ethan groaned, "Are you sure you're up for this?"

"I am," she purred, kissing his other thigh. "And so are you."

His cock stood at full attention, trying its hardest to get noticed by the beautiful woman before him.

She traced a fingertip over his length, and he groaned as she palmed his sack.

He gazed at her wet hair as she leaned in and sucked one ball into her mouth, slid her tongue around it, then let it pop back out again. His cock twitched, tapping against the side of her face as she repeated with the other. She hummed her acknowledgement, then wrapped her hand around him, sliding her mouth up and licking the V of muscle at his juncture.

"Shit, Feya." His fingers sank into her hair, needing more contact.

Her blunt nails slid up and down his thigh while the other pumped him hard.

"Shit," he said again.

Climbing to her feet, she grabbed his hand, and pushed it to her center. She lifted her lips to his ear and whispered, "See what touching you does to me? I need you, Ethan."

As she pulled her mouth from his lobe, he sank his hands into her hair once again and brought his mouth down on hers. Their lips and tongues became a frenzy of movement, and she whimpered, trying to get closer to him.

"Hang on to me," he growled, lifting her. "Wrap your legs around me." He pushed her back against the shower wall and braced her there before reaching down between them and guiding himself to her entrance.

She squirmed, demanding him without words.

He thrust upwards as she ground herself down, and he groaned at the feel of her around him. He kept one arm wrapped under her bottom and braced the other against the wall. She reached up and grabbed at a shelf just above the shower, using it to help maneuver.

He dipped his head and sucked a wet nipple into his mouth, rolling his tongue around it, then nuzzled his nose against it before driving into her. Her breasts bounced as he thrust up. She threw her head back, nearly hitting the wall behind her.

"More," she groaned.

He picked up the pace, bringing his other hand back down to her back side and digging his fingers in.

The sounds she made got him that much more excited, and he could feel his cock thicken and his balls draw up, the tingle of an orgasm building.

He slowed a little, wanting to draw it out long enough for her to gain her own pleasure.

"Don't stop," she gasped. "I'm so close."

He growled again and sped up as she ground herself

against his pelvis. She slid one hand between them and rubbed her bud until she whimpered.

"Oh, god," he moaned, his movement becoming more erratic.

She moaned as her body shuddered, and he grunted with his own release, continuing to pump into her until her insides stopped clenching and his cock ceased its pulsing.

"You feel so good." He dropped his lips to her neck.

"Mmm, so do you." She threaded her fingers in his short hair and pulled his head back so she could kiss him. He moaned as her lips moved against his.

"You trying to kill me?" He slid one hand around her waist and braced with the other against the wall again.

"Maybe." She smiled against his lips.

He laughed, and tilted his head away just enough so he could look at her. "C'mon, let's get you into bed."

He attempted to lift her from his body, but she tightened the hold of her arms and legs. "No."

"Come on, you've got to be exhausted."

She sighed and let her legs drop, and he slid her down his body until they were standing skin to skin.

He reached out and grabbed a towel without looking and wrapped it around her before grabbing one for himself.

She pulled it from her body and blotted her hair. Water dripped down over her breasts then slid down her abdomen.

Ethan's eyes followed the movement, and she giggled.

"What?" he asked, his eyes darting back up to hers.

She leaned in and kissed him softly. "I just like the way you look at me."

"Let's get to bed. You want a tee-shirt to sleep in?" He took her hand and moved backward, leading her out towards the bed.

She shook her head. "I'm happy enough in my skin."

His mouth quirked up. He had absolutely no complaints about her sleeping naked in his bed. "Should I find something to sleep in?"

She scowled at him. "Absolutely not."

"Alright. But you do need to sleep, and so do I." His hand went to his side, which was seeping blood again after their activities.

Her eyes flew to it, and she reached out.

"It was worth it," he said. He grabbed her fingers and kissed them then dug around in his bag for a first aid kit. He found some gauze and some athletic tape and created a clean bandage over the rapidly healing wound.

Moments later, they slid under the blankets together, taking comfort in one another's warmth.

FEYA WOKE ETHAN WITH A SCREAM.

He flew up out of bed, the sheets wet with sap as he flung them back.

She reached for him, hissing in pain. "Take me to the grove. Please Ethan. Take me to my grove."

Ethan didn't bother answering as he shoved his legs into his jeans and scooped her into his arms, sheet and all, then bolted barefoot from the room. He took the stairs at a run then burst out the lobby door. Shouts followed him, but he didn't pay them any attention. Nothing was more important than Feya's suffering at that moment.

He didn't bother with his truck either. He ran through town, down the grove drive, and approached the crew and their worksite.

Feya screamed in his arms as a chainsaw's deafening buzz bit through a sapling.

"What the fuck, Brady?" Brian ran towards him.

As the tree toppled, the pitch of Feya's scream became an inhuman shriek.

"What is that?" Brian's eyes fly to the creature wrapped in a sheet. "What the fuck!"

"She's a dryad," Ethan growled. "You know, the one who's been begging us to stop. She wasn't lying, and she's not delusional."

The chain saw amped up from its idle *wub-wub-wub*, and as the logger fit the spinning chain to the trunk of a tree, Feya screamed again, sobbing. The sheet around her ankles dripped with sap. Moments later, the tree cracked loudly and fell to the ground with a muffled thud, its branches scraping against its neighbors.

Finally understanding, Brian blanched. "Shit."

"You're damn right, shit," Ethan spat, sinking to the ground with his burden so he could tend to her wounds.

Taking a knife from his pocket, he flipped it open and sliced his palm. This was what had done the most good the day before. He lifted the sheet from Feya's ankles and smeared his blood on her wounds, mixing it together with hers. They both clotted immediately.

"Thank you, Ethan, but you can't keep cutting yourself," she whispered, her voice too strained to achieve any volume.

"What can I do?" Brian asked, gripping his hat in his hands as he hunkered down beside them.

"You can stop this." Ethan glared into his eyes.

Brian nodded and jumped to his feet, running and yelling for his men to stop.

The man with the chainsaw was wearing hearing protection and couldn't hear the words.

The saw bit into another tree and Feya's body arched,

her screams pulling everything but the top of her head and the heels of her feet off the ground.

Wild magic crackled in the air then raspberry bushes exploded from the woods, grabbing at the logger and sinking into his flesh. They moved as if sentient, cutting deeper, tearing his skin and exposing muscle. He screamed in pain. Blood spurted from a ripped artery and the vine headed for his eyes, shoving their way in with a wet punch. The screams ended suddenly, and only the scraping and the scratching of the vines could be heard.

"Feya, stop, you have to stop, you're killing him!" Ethan grabbed her shoulders.

She forced herself upright, the sheet pooling to the ground around her. "It's not me!" she cried, witnessing the vines retreat from the man's flesh, leaving him to fall with a wet slap.

The bushes continued flowing from the grove, eating away at the ground. A man who had been running to help bellowed in terror, scrambling to get away.

"Run," Feya whispered. "Tell them to run. The berries don't belong to me. But they have been a part of my grove since the beginning and my power has drawn nature's magic."

Ethan nodded. "You okay for the moment?"

"Go!" she urged, pulling the sheet back up and wiping at her legs with the hem.

Ethan ran towards his coworkers.

"Everybody run! It's not her! She can't stop them!"

Too caught up in the horror before them, the men didn't hear him. The trajectory of the thorns turned towards where they were clustered, the speed of its growth accelerating, and they fled without further prompting.

The raspberries advanced, and Ethan reversed his

direction, scooping Feya back into his arms, wondering if they'd be able to outrun the savage growth.

"Find somewhere to get inside," he shouted over his shoulder. "And tell anyone you see. I don't think they're stopping!"

"I can run on my own." Feya struggled in his arms.

Unprepared, Ethan fumbled her to her feet.

Within a moment, she had the sheet tied like a toga around her body and had girded up the bottom so she could run freely.

"Get whoever you can to safety," she demanded, then sprinted away towards the town.

She ran all the way to Tabby's shop and flew through the door.

"You have to shut down," she gasped, wrenching the door shut behind her. "I'm sorry. I can't stop them."

"Stop what?" Sara hurried from behind the counter to take Feya's hands. "Sweetie, what's going on?"

"The thorns are attacking." Feya pulled her hands away and pointed towards the grove.

"Uh, what?" Sara asked, not understanding.

Feya grabbed her hand and pulled her to the door, down the steps, and across the street.

The raspberries were halfway through the field already.

"Oh shit!" Sara's eyes bulged.

"They already killed a man. One of the loggers that was cutting my trees. But I didn't call them, I swear it to you."

"Okay, okay. Let me get my phone." Sara ran back in and grabbed her cell and purse from behind the counter.

Outside, Ethan screeched to a halt in his beat-up truck.

Feya ran to the door, pulling Sara with her, who was speedily texting a warning to everyone on her town call list.

Her phone rang as she climbed in the truck behind Feya and slammed the door.

"Tabby? Are you okay?" Sara yelled into the phone.

Feya gripped Ethan's arm. "We need to get moving. I don't think we should head back to the hotel."

"We're going to Tabby's," said Sara, dumping her cell into her bag. "It's a little ways out of town."

Ethan rolled down the window and stomped his boot on the gas.

Sara rolled down her window as well and hung half way out, screaming on top of her lungs for everyone to get inside. She waved her arms like a wild woman, until Feya squished out the window beside her to holler, getting as much attention as possible.

They'd all shouted themselves hoarse by the time they pulled into the driveway. Several cars were parked haphazardly in the yard.

Screams rang in the distance as the vines hit downtown and took out anyone who hadn't heeded the warning to get somewhere safe.

Tabby threw open the door and ushered them in.

"That's all of us." She locked the door then handed Ethan a roll of duct tape. "Tape up all the windows that haven't been already. If those thorns hit the house, they could shatter the glass. This will keep things pretty much in place."

Ethan looked down at the tape in his hands and frowned.

Sara patted his shoulder, "I can show you. My parents did it to my windows when I was a kid when we got hit by a hurricane. It keeps glass contained, for the most part."

She peeled the tape loose and slapped it on one corner of the window glass, then smoothed it to the other and ripped the roll free. She made an X then did a few more criss crosses for good measure, creating a sort of childish spiderweb. The whole thing took less than a minute.

"See?" She handed the tape back, then trotted up the stairs for a better vantage point.

Ethan nodded at her retreating form and went to work.

"Feya." Tabby hesitated, biting her lip.

"It's not me," Feya whispered, wishing she didn't have to keep giving the reassurance. She'd never deliberately hurt her new friends. Her enemies, however, she considered fair game.

"Good. That's good. What's doing this then?" asked Tabby.

"It's wild magic. It belongs to the earth herself. The earth does what she sees fit. I am one of her many creatures. I care for her as I can, and I suppose she's returning the favor. One does not tell nature what she can and cannot do."

Tabby nodded then looked down at Feya's scabbed legs and her makeshift toga. "Let's get you cleaned up, okay?"

Feya nodded gratefully, following her friend down the hall.

In the living room, Lucas sat with his arms around a young girl's shoulders. A man, who bore a striking resemblance to the girl, glowered at the young couple from across the room.

Tim sat in a central position on the sofa, ready to step in if need be.

"You stupid child!" The man lunged to his feet. "I told you to drive home."

"And I told you not to follow me!" the girl shouted back.

Lucas looked over and saw his mother escorting Feya. "Welcome back. This is my girlfriend Jenny, and that fine gentleman over there is her father."

15

"We had the pleasure of witnessing the thorn's arrival," said Ethan, then turned to Jenny's father. "Please, try to keep things civil while we're guests in Tabby's house."

Mr. Thompson grumbled about not wanting to be there but not leaving until he had the opportunity to drag his child out— by the hair, if need be.

"I highly suggest you curb that impulse, human," Feya warned, letting go of Ethan and stalking over to the man. "You touch a hair on that child's head, and raspberries will be the least of your worries, understood?"

Ethan took her arm again. "Come on, Feya. I'm sure Jenny's dad won't take any drastic measures under this roof. I'm not opposed to tossing him out on his ass for the thorns to take care of, though."

Luke coughed, covering a laugh. His mother gave him a warning look then led Feya up the stairs.

"Now then, let's get you cleaned up, shall we?" Tabby bustled around, grabbing towels and toiletries, before bringing them to the master bathroom. "I'd say take as long as you need, but I'm not sure how dependable the electricity will be with whatever's coming." She waved a hand towards the front of the house.

"I am sorry," said Feya, accepting the pile of bath supplies and clothes.

Tabby's smile was sad as she patted Feya's arm with a gentle hand. "I in no way blame you. The raspberries aren't yours, right? Just the oaks?"

Feya nodded. "That's right. Well, all the oaks that descend from my original tree. There are a few here and there that I don't have any personal connection with but still have a rapport."

"I'd expect so, sharing land for all these years. Now you just yell if you need anything. I'll be downstairs."

Tabby left Feya to adjust the water temperature so she could oversee the imminent outburst in her living room.

Tim's posture was relaxed as he provided an invisible barrier between the teens and the hot-headed father. He was settled deep in the soft cushions of the couch with his arms crossed over his chest and one ankle resting over the other knee. He appeared for all the world as if this were any other day in his girlfriend's home.

Tabby settled next to him and kissed his cheek.

Ethan continued lurking in the doorway, which grabbed her attention.

"Ethan, please sit. Relax. There really isn't much more to do at the moment other than wait. And thank you for taping so quickly."

"Thank me again when you have to get it all off," he joked, pushing from the door frame and taking a seat opposite Tim.

Tabby smiled and raised her eyebrows. "That's why God created the people who invented razor blades and Goo Gone."

That earned her a laugh from Lucas.

The lights flickered, and Jenny flinched. Luke wrapped his arm tighter around her shoulders. A shriek from upstairs told them that Feya had gotten a blast of cold water.

"Lucas, honey, would you mind filling up the downstairs bathtub?" Tabby glanced at him, noting his tense frame. "Jenny, you come with me and help me make sure we have all the candles, batteries, and flashlights on hand that we'll need." She held her hand out to the girl as her son wordlessly stalked out of the room.

Jenny hurried towards her, her eyes dashing from her boyfriend's retreating back to her father.

The three adult men sat in stony silence, listening to the hustle and bustle going on in the house around them.

Running water and low voices were punctuated by distant screams and the rumbling and rustling of the approaching doom.

Everything stopped. The water quit running. The lights flickered off. Dead silence filled the air like a held breath. And then it released. The windows rattled, the house shook, and the ground heaved like an earthquake rippling all around.

Feya ran down the stairs, her hair dripping wet, dressed in clean leggings and a baggy sweater. Tabby and Jenny dashed in from the kitchen, clutching each other for support.

Hissing and scraping assaulted the house. Things slithered all over the outside, eliciting sharp squeals from the glass. Jenny ran to Luke, huddling in his arms as her eyes flew wildly in every direction.

A muffled, "Whoa!" from Sara could just be heard over the pandemonium.

Feya strode towards the windows as they creaked and

cracked, shards of glass held in place by the spiderwebs of duct tape Ethan had applied only minutes before.

Thorny vines blocked light from entering. They were unlike anything any of them had ever seen before. These weren't the raspberry plants that had just begun budding out with leaves and the promise of flowers. These bore vines as thick as a man's arm. Thorns, wicked and sharp, protruded from all angles. Giant leaves like something from a prehistoric rainforest burst out and blotted what little light had been able to eke its way through.

Behind Feya, Tabby flipped on a flashlight and gaped at the sight before them.

As suddenly as it started, the shaking and the noise settled.

Feya's hand went to the glass, as if to touch the vine encasing the house.

"I think it's done. At least for now." She pulled back and headed for the front door.

"Uh, where are you going?" Tabby asked, hurrying after her;

Before anyone could catch up to her, she yanked the door open. "To see." A wall of greenery blocked the outside. She turned and headed back to the living room.

"Still got that knife?" she asked Ethan, holding a hand out palm up.

He pulled it out and popped it open. "Here. But I think it's too small to accomplish much."

"Do you think a chainsaw would be okay?" Luke asked.

Feya shrugged. "They're not connected to a dryad, so I'd guess it wouldn't cause any true pain."

"I'll be right back then." He headed for the basement, Jenny hot on his heels.

Tim put up a hand to stop Carl Thompson from following. "There isn't anything you can do."

"She's my child. I can do whatever I want," he growled, pushing against Tim, trying to get him to move out of his way. Tim stood his ground, solid as a wall.

"And this, again, is my house," said Tabby. "Lucas turns 18 tomorrow. And Jenny already is. They're adults. They have to make their own choices and deal with whatever consequences come their way."

Thompson grunted and headed back to the living room, the glint in his eyes making Tabby uncomfortable.

Tim drew a comforting arm around Tabby, and kissed the top of her head. "I'll do whatever I can to keep our kids safe."

The words struck Tabby, that Tim considered Lucas his, which now extended to Jenny.

"I love you." She lifted her head to kiss his cheek. "And it seems like Lucas has always been yours."

"I love you both with all my heart, and if Luke loves Jenny, then I do too. She's family now." Tim gave her one more squeeze then went to inspect the windows for damage.

The two teens reemerged. Luke set the chainsaw down, checked over the chain, made sure there was gas in the tank, and started it up.

Feya flinched away at the rumble.

Ethan put his arms around her and murmured into her hair. "Shh, it's not for you. You're safe."

She nuzzled into him, and he shifted her head so one ear settled against his chest over his heart and he could cover the other with his hand.

Listening to the steady beat, she blocked out the noise.

Fresh vegetal smells filled the air as Lucas cleared the doorway, then stepped outside.

"Whoa."

Feya wriggled free and followed, now more able to handle the wub-wub-wub of the saw.

Vines covered everything, bearing immense thorns and large buds just about ready to burst into bloom. They wound through yards, though only minimally invaded the streets, the asphalt an adequate deterrent. It crossed roads but didn't consume them.

"I wonder how big the raspberries will be," Tim mused, avoiding stabbing his shoulder on a thorn by mere inches.

Tabby smiled at him. "Only you could find the bright side of this one."

DURING THE LATE AFTERNOON, others began emerging from homes and businesses, checking in on each other as Oak Grove citizens were like to do.

Well, perhaps not the mayor.

Fredrick was pacing the halls of his office, snapping at anyone who dared look in his direction. He'd, of course, been indoors during the rage of the vegetation that now owned the town. He had no computer, the phones were down, and to top it all off, there wasn't any electricity.

He'd watched out of the third story window as vines had crawled up telephone poles, ripping the lines and toppling everything to the ground in a mangled mess. His secretary assured him there were no live wires. The windows, despite the height of the building housing his office, were completely smothered in greens.

"That stupid creature ruined everything," he ranted, dashing papers off his desk with an open palm.

"Now, Freddy, I don't think you can blame this on a

creature, this is more of an act of god, wouldn't you say?" A soft sweet voice attempted to sooth him.

"Mary?" he spun to face his wife. "How did you get in here? Are you alright?"

She hurried over and threw her arms around him. "I'm fine, darling. The neighbor boy helped get me out and brought me over here on his four wheeler."

Fred chuckled at the thought of his wife on the back of a four wheeler in her long gray skirt and delicate white blouse. "I'm glad you're okay. But really, you shouldn't be out in this. What if something happened to you?"

She tipped up onto her toes and kissed his cheek. "Nonsense. It's just a few plants. I bet all we need is a few drums of weed killer. I'll see what I can do. In the meantime, let's go to your office. There's nothing to be done at the moment, so let's spend some quality time together, shall we?"

She raised her eyebrows, blushing at her own innuendo.

JERRY HAD TAKEN A SICK DAY. Fat lot of good that had done him since now the whole town was shut down. He glowered up at the towering oaks in his front yard, completely untouched by the thorns.

"Mess with the big dogs and you get the teeth," he grumbled, heading for his tool shed. He flipped the light switch then cursed, it seemed the electricity wasn't coming back any time soon.

An electric Coleman lantern sat covered in dust, but it still worked when he turned the knob. It threw weak light, but it was enough to locate his long, round files. He settled a chain on his lap and began rasping it over a link, sharpening its wicked teeth.

PASTOR RACHELLE ATTEMPTED to cut through the vines with heavy old rusty loppers with very little success. Not knowing what else to do, she fell to her knees and cast her eyes to the ceiling.

"Lord, I don't know what your will is on this one, but please let my little flock be safe. Please, let there be none injured. Well, I know there won't be none. I heard those screams, Lord. How did this happen? I know Feya didn't do this. This is raspberry bramble, not oak trees. I don't know what else to do. Please lord, keep me safe, help me find a way to help others. Please use these hands however possible."

She would have continued, but a loud buzzing interrupted her, and then the foyer doors burst open.

"Rachelle! Are you okay?"

"Oh! Bill! Thank you, Jesus. Oh you are just an answer to prayer. Yes. I'm okay. You? Beverly?" She used the edge of a pew to help her to her feet.

Bill rushed over and took her hands. "We're all fine. We're just trying to check on everyone we can. Actually, there are a few injured. Could we bring them here? The hospital is too far away—"

"Yes, bring them," she interrupted. "It is the duty of the church to take care of its community. And it is my pleasure to be the helping hands the Lord uses. I've got simple first aid supplies, and there's plenty of food in the pantry. We just don't have a way to cook it."

"Don't worry about that. Greyson opened the general store to us. There's a lot of prepackaged stuff, including those MRE's he's got stashed in the back. He figures this is an emergency. And besides, there's no way he's going to get shipments when the roads are like they are now. But it's just a few of us, at least right now. We want to make sure our resources don't go to waste, especially the fresh stuff.

"Well then. What are we waiting for?" Rachelle threw her arms wide. "Bring them in."

THE TREE GAVE A MIGHTY CRACK, then fell to the ground, bouncing slightly before lying still.

Jerry thrust his fists into the air in triumph then turned to the second tree.

FEYA FELL down Tabby's front steps. The skin of her ankles split with fresh wounds, and she screamed.

Tabby, Luke, Tim, and Ethan ran to her, falling to their knees around her.

She raised her shaking hand towards Ethan, and he gathered her into his lap, once again pulling the knife from his pocket and sliced his hand open.

Tabby gasped at the sight, before collecting herself and dashing back into the house to grab water and towels.

Sara threw open a second story window that the vines missed and leaned out. "Is she okay?"

Luke looked up at her and shook his head. "Mom's inside looking for first aid stuff, I think."

Sara disappeared again, presumably to help.

Tim knelt by Ethan. "Let me help." He touched a hand to Feya's forehead. "I'm going to straighten your legs, okay?"

She nodded, and bit her lip as he gently took one ankle in his hands and slowly stretched it out, then held it steady while Ethan worked.

Shouts that sounded like Jenny and her father rang from inside the house.

Luke's eyes flew toward the sound and Tim touched his shoulder. "We're fine, you get in there."

Luke was up and running before the words even left Tim's mouth.

By the time Tabby returned with Sara in tow, Feya was sobbing and clinging to Ethan, but her wounds had sealed themselves with ugly scabs. Ethan waved them over. "She could use a drink of water, but I'm going to carry her out back to the trees. It'll help her to be close to them."

Tabby nodded mutely and headed back inside to grab some water bottles, while Ethan carried Feya to the stand of oaks.

As she turned, she witnessed Carl Thompson shove his daughter out the door.

"Get moving, we're leaving this hell hole. I don't care if we have to walk all the way out of town. We're going." He gave a brutal yank to her arm.

"Daddy, no!" she sobbed, trying to escape his iron grip.

"You'll do what I say," he snarled.

"Mr. Thompson, stop. Please, just leave Jenny with us. I promise I'll keep her safe." Luke ran out of the house after them.

Tim jumped to his feet, preparing to intervene.

"Safe?" the man yelled. "Safe?" he flung his arms wide, still clutching his daughter's arm and causing her to fall.

There was a pop, and Jenny screamed, crumpling as tears streamed down her cheeks.

"You son of a bitch!" Luke shouted, running towards them.

But even he wasn't fast enough.

Thompson was standing near the only oak tree in the front yard when he'd dislocated his daughter's shoulder.

Its branches lashed out, and Feya burst from the bark, sinking her fingers into his chest, cracking his ribs wide open. With a squelch, she pulled his still beating heart from him and threw it to the ground, stamping one bare foot down on it.

The heart exploded, spraying blood all over Feya and Jenny, while Thompson's body fell to the ground with a dull thud. Feya's head tilted to the side, as if surveying her handiwork, her eyes unfocused, emotionless, and alien. Blood ran from her empty upraised hand, down her arm, and over her bare breast. She brought her hand down, and wiped it absently on her thigh.

16

Tabby watched in horror as Jenny wiped at her blood-splattered face with the edge of her sleeve.

Feya emitted a harsh shriek, reabsorbing back into the tree, no longer in control of her impulses, her rage now all consuming.

Luke ran to his girlfriend, gathered her in his arms, and carried her inside.

"I'm going to see if I can help," said Sara from the doorway, then followed them.

Tabby gave the corpse a vicious kick with the toe of her boot, then looked up at Tim and Ethan. "What?"

"That was…" Tim struggled to find words.

"Extreme?" Ethan supplied. "I think everything that has happened to Feya lately has been extreme. She woke after over 100 years of slumber, was thrust into the modern world, learned how to live in it, and then came under attack by the very people she was supposed to be safe with."

Tim sighed. "Not exactly what I meant. I meant you, Tabby. Way to kick a man when he's down."

She harrumphed and crossed her arms.

"What should we do with the body? Report it to the police?" Ethan asked, hesitating to even suggest it.

"I don't think so. What are we going to say? An earth goddess murdered him?" Tabby stared down at Carl Thompson's pale corpse.

"We should probably bury him. It isn't like EMS can deal with this right now. If need be, we'll let the authorities know when this whole mess is cleared up."

As if in response, several roots from the oak thrust their way up out of the ground, wrapped around the body, and yanked it under the soil, leaving only bloodstains behind.

Ethan stared, dumbfounded. Had that been Feya? The tree? It was hard to tell. He had seen her trees act on their own in the interest of their mother before.

Tabby blew out a breath and headed indoors. Tim followed close behind, taking her hand as they went.

Her son had his girl seated on the counter and was gently washing her skin clean with a bottle of water and a wad of paper towels.

He looked up at her entry. "Mom, can Jenny borrow some clothes?"

"Of course. They'll be a little big, but at least they're clean." Tabby turned her attention to the girl. "Grab whatever you like. Don't worry about pawing through my drawers."

Jenny nodded, not looking her in the eye.

"Are you going to be alright? Do you need anything else?" Tabby asked, placing one hand on her son's shoulder and the other on the girl's uninjured one.

Jenny shook her head.

Sara plopped at old, slightly cobwebby sling on the counter. "Found this in your basement, Tabby. Hope you don't mind my poking around."

After Tabby shook her head, Sara turned back to Jenny. "I'm by no means an expert, but I think we need to get that shoulder popped back in."

Jenny's eyes were wide, but she pulled her lips between her teeth and nodded.

"Tim, can you hold her still? I've only seen this on TV, but we've got to try." As Tim took position, arms tight around the girl while Luke held her hand, she grasped the younger woman's arm, holding it at a 90 degree angle, then slowly began pulling.

Jenny gasped as her shoulder slid back into place with a pop.

"There we go. Now let's get this sling on you and you can rest." Sara remained with the pair to help get the girl settled.

"All right then," said Tabby. "I'm going to make my way to town and see what we can do to help."

Tim grabbed her hands. "I'll go with you. I'll bring the loppers, just in case."

Ethan remained still, his hands shoved deep in his pockets, a dazed expression glazing his face. Tabby lay a gentle hand on his bicep. He blinked a couple of times then clenched his jaw.

"Would you like to come with us?"

He nodded, then pulled his hands out and swiped them over his jeans.

The trio made their way across what used to be the lawn, carefully traversing over and around the thick vines and thorns. For the most part, the loppers were useless, unable to open wide enough to fit around the plant.

An elderly woman popped her head out of her second story window, "I don't suppose you could give an old lady a hand?"

"I've got this," said Ethan. "I'll catch up later." He

headed towards the house, introduced himself, then climbed in an open window on the first floor that was only partially covered.

Tabby and Tim continued. Normally, the walk would have been about ten minutes, but with such a change in terrain, it was more like half an hour as they had to double back from time to time to find a clearer route.

They were joined by several other families making their way to downtown Oak Grove.

The massive vines covered buildings on all sides, some having actually broken windows and made it inside businesses and apartments. A coat of mud covered almost everything. A box truck, flipped on its side, was surrounded by people with saws and axes. The shattering of glass and the grateful sobs of the man inside, made Tabby's heart speed up. How many more of her friends and neighbors were trapped inside vehicles, houses, or businesses?

Tabby scraped her palms several times on the thorns and bits of shattered glass, the deep scratches leaking blood, as she made her way to The Sip Down. The big window out front was gone, and a thick layer of vines had poured inside.

She continued scrambling, calling for Bill.

From down the road, she heard him yell, "I'm fine, but I've got a few employees in there who need help. Has anyone seen my sister?"

A muffled shout came from the back. Looking around for something to cut with, Tabby found a bread knife and began sawing away at the limbs blocking the back room.

Tim followed a few minutes later, having acquired a small hack saw, and attacked the plants right alongside her.

It took only a few minutes to cut enough away to get to the door, which thankfully was set up to swing inward.

"Oh, thank God." Grace, one of the baristas scrambled out then held out both hands to another young woman and a teenage boy, helping them out.

"I thought no one was going to come." The girl's breath came out in pants and shudders. "We tried to rip through it with our hands, but that shit is tough."

The other young woman nodded in agreement.

Tabby handed over the bread knife. "This was my convenient weapon. Why don't you see what you can salvage here."

A gleeful cackle was muffled by the wall shared with Beverly's Brew House, followed by a puff of smoke. "Take that you thorny bitches!" A baseball bat exploded through the drywall, giving the smoke a larger escape route. Bev smashed the bat against the wall a few more times, until the hole was big enough to climb through.

"Howdy!" She called brightly, brandishing a bottle of Polish vodka bearing a white label with bright green print .

"Sis, are you drunk?" Bill moved to help her climb over, but Bev tumbled through before he could get his hands on her.

"You betcha!" She took a swig, gargled it, then spit it back through the hole, speedily setting the airborne alcohol aflame with a lighter.

"You're going to burn the place down!" He pushed her out of the way and scrambled through the hole, doing his best to beat the blazing thorns into nothingness.

Giggling, Bev followed him back through, repeating the production.

Banging, cursing, and more smoke followed as Tabby and the other onlookers, scrambled to look inside the burning bar.

Smoke rolled around, breezing through any opening it could find, but most of the fire had done its job already. The counter, table tops, chairs, stools—just about everything—was covered in remnants of vines. The bar itself wasn't in all that bad of shape.

"You've been busy, it seems," Tabby commented, yanking at a blackened branch that easily came away. While the table underneath was certainly scorched, that was the worst of it.

"Yep. Drinks anyone? It's on the house." Bev thrust the bottle of rum into the air, causing a small amount to splash out.

Snorting a laugh, Tabby shook her head. "Maybe later. The laugh was good enough for now. Thanks for that."

"Don't encourage her," Bill muttered, finding a smoldering bit of plant matter and stamping it out. "Where's John at?"

"Home with a cold. So our little friend, Feya, do all this?" Bev asked, following the group as they made their way back out to the streets.

"Not exactly." Tabby filled her in on everything she knew.

"That rat bastard had it coming. It's all Fred-dick's fault. Stupid mornon—moreen—more—"

"Okay, sis, give it a rest." Bill wrapped an arm around her shoulders.

"No!" she shouted. "I will not be silenced! My voice will be heard. Mayor dick-head is reshponsidle—respon-ci-ble for this!"

Others in the streets cheered for her and shouted their own obscenities at the mayor who was still holed up in his office.

"Town meeting time! Bar's open!" Bev about-faced and swung the heavy front door open. It, apparently, had not handled her ministrations so well, as it fell from the frame and landed on the sidewalk with a thud.

"Hell yeah!" someone called back, and the crowd

followed her inside. They had to break the burnt vine, but it was quick work with many helping hands.

FREDRICK, his wife, and the rest of his office followed the raucous sounds to the bar.

"Unbelievable," Mary scoffed. "Partying at a time like this."

Jerry moved ahead of them, wielding a chainsaw and clearing a path for them down the middle of the road.

Once at the bar, Mary waltzed in like she owned the place.

Hands on her hips, eyes narrowed, lips pursed, she listened in on the unsanctioned meeting for just a minute before speaking up. "Ahem. The mayor has arrived, I suggest you give him your attention."

The crowd turned, many an eyebrow raised, and gawked at her. Mary had never set foot in the brew house before, so it was something like an ostrich wandering into a wolf den.

She clung to her husband's elbow as they made their way forward, quiet chatter following in their wake.

Fredrick cleared his throat and squared his shoulders. "There's no reason to beat around the bush. This is all because of that creature. Now, I might not have believed in the town folk story before, but I certainly do now, and it seems there is much history has left out. She is a menace, and the sooner we can bring her to justice, the better."

A loud crack interrupted whatever he was going to say next, and a tree root burst through the floor. From it rose Feya, looking like a true wild creature straight out of mythology.

"Justice you say? Was it justice to destroy my trees? Was

it justice to ignore my every warning? This was my home for hundreds of years before a human ever stepped foot on this soil. I am justice. The oaks are my home, my offspring, my very soul. The vines are their own beings, but we have lived in peace for centuries. Your desecration of my home was also of theirs. I have no influence over them—"

A chainsaw roared, and Jerry sprinted for her. He nearly brought it down on the root when she grabbed his face in her hands, her fingers growing longer and twig-like, pushing into his ears, nose, and eyes. The chainsaw hit the ground, still whining. Someone made a grab for it, but another root shot out of the earth and slammed down on it, smashing it with the force of a semi-truck. Metal bits rained down in its wake.

Jerry's head exploded under the pressure of Feya's fingers. Bits of blood, brain, and other tissue flew in all directions as the dryad ripped the man's head apart.

More roots shoved their way through the floor, knocking people over in the turmoil, and yanked the body into the ground.

"Monster! Demon!" Mary shrieked, pointing a manicured finger at the blood drenched tree fae.

Feya's head whipped around, and a hiss like wind through leaves burst from her lips as she stalked towards the screaming woman.

Fredrick grabbed his wife around the middle and hauled her out the door, up a set of thorny stairs, and broke his way into an overhead apartment. Lucky for them, it was empty.

"I'll end that creature, I promise you that." He gathered her close as she shook in his arms.

Down below in the bar, Feya's wild green eyes flitted around the room until they landed on a familiar face.

"Ethan?" she whispered, cocking her head to the side.

With a jerky movement, she separated from the root, and ran towards him.

Men and women scrambled out of her way, and a few shouted at Ethan to move.

Her inhuman movements ceased a hair's breadth from his nose, her toes touching the tips of his boots. She sniffed, lifting her long-fingered hand to stroke his cheek, leaving a crimson streak in its wake.

Her eyes focused on that trail of blood, and her fingers retracted until they appeared human once more.

"Ethan," she whispered again, seeming to come to herself a little more.

Ethan shrugged out of the flannel button down he'd borrowed from Lucas, and gently pulled it around her shoulders. He tugged her into his arms, murmuring in her ear so only she could understand.

She nodded, slipping her arms into the sleeves of the shirt, then buttoned it before taking Ethan's hand and leaving the bar.

The crowd of humans parted, allowing them to leave.

17

Ethan woke before dawn with Feya slumbering peacefully in his arms in the middle of her grove. It was the most comforting place he could think to take her and the safest for everyone else.

They were both caked with blood and dirt, not having had the chance to wash up.

Feya muttered, then slowly blinked her eyes open.

She sprang to her feet. "Oh no." She spun in a circle. "Oh no, no, no, no—"

Ethan stood and pulled her into his arms. "What is it? What's wrong?" He stroked her hair and kissed the top of her head.

"So many trees. I know I lost control, but I didn't think I'd gone this far." She peeked over his shoulder. Her brows furrowed as she frowned.

Ethan pulled away, and tilted her chin up so she was looking him in the eye. "Feya, this isn't new, this is your grove. I brought you out here after… after yesterday."

"Oh," she whispered, then ducked and pressed her forehead to his shoulder.

He chuckled and dipped so he could place a light kiss on her dark lips.

She sank into him, forgetting everything else for just a moment, letting the sensation of him waft over her skin.

"Feya, hold on a moment." Ethan pulled back again as her touch became more enthusiastic. "As much as I'm craving you right now, we need to get cleaned up." He rubbed at the dirt on her cheek.

She looked down at her hands, momentarily shocked by the dried blood caked around her fingertips.

"Oh." She scrubbed her fingers together in an attempt to rid herself of the grime.

"Is there a stream or something around here?" he asked, taking her hands and kissing the backs of them.

She blinked, scrunching her eyebrows again. "Of course."

His own brows rose, waiting.

"Who ever heard of a grove springing up away from a water source? Come on." She turned her hand in his, gripping it, and pulled him through the trees.

As the road cleared, many families in the town could be seen stuffing themselves into their vehicles with everything they could possibly fit. It was all too much for some people.

EMS was noticeably absent. With the phones down, they couldn't be called. Instead, those injured that had survived the raspberry attack were ferried by their neighbors to the local hospital or the church.

As word spread around outside of Oak Grove, a fleet of deputy sheriffs made their way into town and were immediately flagged down by the mayor. A few made their way to his office while the others spread around town to find out exactly what was happening. Eventually, they left bewildered, not having met Feya themselves and coming to no logical conclusion for what they were seeing. They were having trouble communicating with their radios but promised to return soon with more help.

After the last taillight disappeared in the distance, the ground at the edge of town billowed upwards in an explosion of plants, effectively cutting off the roads in and out.

The air crackled with magic, disrupting GPS and radio signals, and muddling the minds of the deputies so they couldn't quite remember what they'd seen or who they'd talked to. In fact, they couldn't remember they'd ever been to Oak Grove once they arrived home and settled in with friends and family for the evening.

Inside the town, people gathered, inspecting the aftermath of the explosion of vegetation and feeling the difference in the air.

"Someone find me that creature!" Mayor Alcroft's face shone beet red as he whirled away from the sight. He and Mary had left their little hidey-hole during the interaction.

A few men nodded and shouldered rifles, but others, including Bill, Beverly, and Lucas blocked their way.

Rachelle stepped forward. "Feya is our dryad, and it's your fault all of this happened."

Fredrick sputtered and cursed under his breath. "You're supposed to be a woman of God. How dare you stand up for this pagan interloper!"

Rachelle's eyebrows rose. "Pagan? Honestly, we've not had the chance to chat about religion, but how dare you assume that you know everything about God's creation. Feya is as much a part of this place as any of us. More so, in fact, since she was here before us."

"I think you need to step out of our way." One of the men lifted his gun to his shoulder. "There's no reason anyone else has to get hurt. Once we put down the creature, we can get this town back to normal."

"Absolutely not. Lower that gun Lincoln Meyer. I've never known you to be a violent man."

Instead of lowering it, he took aim. "That was before my home was destroyed and my wife was killed. Now move."

No one witness Fredrick and Mary walking away. All were consumed by the confrontation unfolding before them.

"I'm sorry about Vanessa—"

BANG!

Rachelle's eyes flew wide as she landed in a heap.

The people surrounding them sprang into action. Bill tackled Lincoln, taking him to the ground, his gun flying from his hands, only to be picked up by Bev, who immediately checked it over before aiming it back at him.

More shots rang, and shouts followed. The pandemonium of neighbor fighting neighbor raged around Rachelle as blood spilled from her body.

Lucas grabbed her up in his arms, and attempted to stop the flow.

She reached a bloodied hand up and patted his cheek. "You're a good man, Lucas. You take care now." Her hand fell as her eyes lost focus and her chest ceased to move.

Lucas set her gently on her back and attempted CPR. There was no one to help him as he fought for the minister's life. A woman who'd been so important to her community, had been so kind to those in need, was gone for good. Feya hadn't been able to keep her promise.

18

Bev's nose was broken. She'd fired the rifle several times after retrieving the remaining bullets from Meyer's pocket, and then someone had popped her a good one in the face. She didn't know who'd done it, and during the chaos, no one else did either.

Luke continued cradling Rachelle's body, rocking the limp form as if comforting her.

"Come on, sweetheart." Tabby rested a hand on her son's shoulder. "You've done all you can. She's gone."

Bill bent, lifting the body in his arms, and headed to the church.

Luke allowed his mother to help him to his feet, his puffy red face covered in tears.

Jenny and Sara met them near the end of their road astride the four wheeler, Jenny's arm still supported by a sling. When she took in her boyfriend's face, she stumbled from her seat and ran into his arms, not caring that he was still covered in someone's blood. He clung to her and sobbed into her hair as her fingers clutched at the back of his tee-shirt, assuring him that she was in this with him.

"I'm going to go help Bill," said Sara quietly, then followed his retreating form on foot.

A warm arm fell around Tabby's shoulders, and she looked up into Tim's solemn countenance, traces of tears lingering on his cheeks. She reached up and brushed at a trail with her thumb, leaving a streak of dirt behind.

"Well, I suppose there wasn't much I could do to help anyhow," she said.

He pulled her into his chest and kissed her hair. "You do plenty, love. More than you even know. Should I take you home?"

She nodded against him, then pulled back, taking his hands in hers. "And I want it to be your home too."

"I'd like that very much." He kissed her tenderly, then followed the kids back to the house on foot.

FEYA STOOD ALONE at the edge of her territory, having left Ethan helping out with organizing the available food.

Wild magic whipped around her in whirlwind and she accepted it into her, letting it twine with her own, making her something new. Something more.

She'd shed her modern apparel and glamoured forth a style of dress fashionable hundreds of years ago. She'd worn something very much like it when she was young, before the seed of her grove trees had traveled over oceans to the wild lands. It was green and gold and soft against her skin. On her brow rested a circlet of silver and emerald. She was done pretending. It was time to be exactly who she was always meant to be.

She'd dealt in kindness for long enough. Justice and judgment were now hers to wield as queen—as goddess. Her trees had risen to her bidding and the land had followed suit. The static crackle of the magic shield that now surrounded her kingdom answered the power within her. The land was hers and she was the land's.

The wild magic settled in like it was always meant for her.

Footsteps approached, but she didn't turn. He would have to come to her, even without her silent call.

Brian Fuller, the man in charge of the logging operation that had brought her to power, fell to his knees in the dirt.

"Ma'am, I've come to beg for your forgiveness."

She turned then, finally giving him her attention. She stepped forward and touched the crown of his bent head. "You shall have it. You were following orders. Granted, they were orders from foul evil men, but it was your job, I suppose. I can forgive, but I will not forget, I'm afraid."

He turned his face up to her. "What can I do to make things right?"

"Do? What's done is done. But I could use your service, if you are willing."

He nodded.

"You are well versed in forests, yes?"

Again, he nodded.

"Then you will gather trusted men and patrol the woods. Keep track of where animals nest, what trees are dying, and keep watch on the barrier. Will you do this?"

"Yes ma'am."

She held up a hand in correction. "Goddess."

"Goddess?"

She nodded once. "Yes. Until we get on more familiar terms and I can discern if you are fully to be trusted. You may go now."

"Yes ma'—I mean, Goddess." He flushed and cast his eyes to the forest floor.

She waved him off, turning back to the barrier to study her work once more. She could feel every tree, sapling, root, branch, and elder oak, as if members of her physical body. She was the forest. She would rule her land now, and no one would ever hurt her again.

FREDRICK WAS STILL MUTTERING obscenities as he threw open his front door, Mary following behind him.

"I'll show that little bitch. I'll cut down every tree myself if I have to, but her time is up." He yanked his tie loose and threw it to the ground.

"Freddy, what are you going to do? You can't go around cutting trees, not at your age. You don't know what you're doing." Mary stuck to him like a shadow.

"It doesn't matter. All I need to do is kill the damn things." He stomped towards the basement, yanking on the light chain, having forgotten the electricity was out. "God-damn it!"

Mary hurried back into the kitchen and grabbed a flashlight.

He didn't even thank her as he grabbed it and continued his descent into the darkness. In the far corner, covered in cobwebs, was the chainsaw his son had bought him before moving away, stating that he'd have to do his own yard work now. He hadn't seen the ungrateful shit in 20 years.

Grabbing an old stick of wood, he lashed the webs away and hefted the machine shoved the little bottle of oil sitting next to it into his back pocket. He really didn't know anything about chainsaws, but he could figure it out as he went.

He stomped back up the stairs, Mary still trailing him, wringing her hands.

"Would you stop your fussing woman. Stay in the house."

In the garage, he found a fish tank siphon with a hand pump, left over from his son's childhood.

He carried both out to the driveway where his car was parked and set them on the ground just under the fuel door. He dumped the contents of the oil container into the saw then, using one blunt finger, he flipped open the gas tank door, unscrewed the cap, and slithered one end of the siphon into the tank, fitting the other to the chainsaw. He squeezed the pump hard, and the gas quickly flowed from tank to tank, making a mess all over the driveway.

He yanked the pull cord starter, and the thing didn't even cough. He muttered darkly under his breath, pulling a few more times until it finally rumbled its protest at life.

The large oak in his front yard was his first target. It was Mary's favorite tree for the shade it offered the front of the house all summer long, but that was just too bad.

It was harder than he'd thought, holding the spinning chain to the trunk of the tree, chips of wood flying every which way, but he managed. The tree groaned then began to crack. He backed away, still holding the running saw. He turned, ready to target another tree.

He didn't see Feya appear out of the falling oak, didn't see her touch a finger to it, didn't see it switch the direction of its fall.

The only warning he received was the shadow and the whoosh as the tree slammed down on top of him, knocking him so he fell on top of the saw as it continued running, his finger pinned between the ground and the trigger. He screamed as the chain cut into his belly, he begged for mercy as it bit into his organs, whimpered as it severed his spinal column, then lay twitching in the grass, bits of skin and guts surrounding him as the ever-present buzz of the saw whirred on.

A shadow fell over him, viewing his mangle body. Feya reached down and shut off the saw, then squatted beside him. "Now it is your body that will nourish my trees. Your sacrifice is greatly appreciated." She patted his cheek in an almost affectionate manner as his last spark of life snuffed out.

Mary came running from the house, screaming like a banshee.

Feya tapped herself on the chin with one bloody finger, raising her eyes in thought. "Yes, that would be a fitting end to the murderer's mate."

Mary dropped to her knees, still wailing. Feya knelt beside her, taking the old woman's face in her hands. "Mourn your mate's demise. Mourn every loss of life. From now on until the end of time, you'll always be first to know of an impending death, and you shall mourn for every dying and lost soul."

She opened her mouth so wide it looked as if her jaw unhinged and breathed a noxious, black mist into Mary's gaping mouth.

Mary's face grew gaunt and stretched beyond the natural, her chin dropping long and low. Her eyes glazed into a glowing white. Her skin shriveled and shrank until it clung to her bones. Her hair fell out in clumps around her, littering the lawn like spent dandelion fluff. Her fingers, gnarled and boney, grew sharp black claws from their tips, as did her toes inside her now too-big shoes.

Her scream took on an eerie quality, and she rose to her feet to begin wandering the yard.

Feya stopped her with a touch. "You will mourn this man no longer. Now go, spirit of the forest. Seek shelter and make your home there. You will know when your call is needed next."

The distended jaw snapped shut, and the skin drooped now that it was no longer stretched, flapping below her chin.

The thing that was Mary scuttled to the woods, leaving behind her shoes, her husband's body, and her humanity.

Feya would see to it that she remained clothed, fed, and adequately sheltered. The newborn banshee had an important job to do, after all.

19

Two days passed and the full moon overtook the sky. Brian, along with his select group of guardians, lost time as if they'd become blackout drunk without the party.

He awoke naked, surrounded by his men, and immediately knew something changed. He lifted a hand to scrub over his face, and found he'd grown a short beard. As he pulled his fingers away, his eyes landed on his nails, which had blackened and sharpened into points. Down at the creek, he caught his distorted reflection in the moving water. His blue eyes had turned as amber as honey.

Feya appeared carrying a backpack full of men's sweatpants.

"Good, you're awake. You've all taken to the magic of the forest quite well, I see." She patted a nearby man's back as if stroking a dog.

"What happened to us?" Brian asked, gratefully accepting a pair of the sweats and yanking them up his legs.

"Losing time around every full moon is now your

norm. You'll also notice an excessive amount of hair, and you'll start shedding."

"Are you saying we're, uh, we're..." Brian struggled to accept the words that were running through his head.

"Werewolves, yes. The perfect predator and the perfect guardians. Lead your pack well, alpha."

A moment later, Ethan rumbled out of the tree line on a four-wheeler, hauling bags of supplies for the new pack. Sara rode another, equally burdened.

"Ethan!" Brian jogged forward. "I've been wondering what had happened to you. Are you okay?"

"I'm fine." Ethan gripped his former boss's hand in a firm shake. "I see you've made peace with my mate."

"Your mate?" Brian raised an eyebrow.

"Feya." He nodded towards her.

"The Goddess is your mate?"

"Yes, I guess she is a goddess, isn't she?" Ethan glanced to where Feya stood talking quietly with a few of the men, while Sara passed around the backpacks full of supplies.

"And what the hell? Turn your head," Brian demanded, stepping into his space.

Ethan whipped his head to the side, thinking maybe there was a creepy crawler making its way up his neck. "What? What?"

"You're ears are fucking pointy!"

"Yeah. Apparently, I'm an elf." Ethan shrugged.

Brian's eyebrows furrowed. "You mean she turned you into an elf?"

Ethan shook his head. "Nah. I've always been one."

"Huh. You've always been a little different, I just thought it was a culture thing," said Brian.

Ethan smiled. "It's probably a little of both. So how are you guys holding up? Are you good with your choice?"

Brian's face took on an animalistic quality. "So far, it's

fantastic. This werewolf thing is going to take some getting used to, though."

"Don't you have any family or anything?" Ethan kept his voice low. Feya was across the clearing, continuing to hand out supplies.

Eyes down cast, Brian shook his head. "Not really. Divorced, no kids. I'm an only child, and my parents live in Florida, so I don't see them very often, but I would like to visit them from time to time."

"So long as you remain loyal, that can be arranged." Feya appeared at Ethan's side.

Brian gave a startled snarl and immediately shame overcame him. This was his mistress, and aggression towards her was unacceptable.

"It's okay, wolf. You're still learning. I'll try to make my presence known sooner next time." She placed a gentle hand on his arm, earning a grin in return.

She turned and faced the rest of the pack. "I'll be heading into town soon and I'd like you there with me, minus one or two to keep patrolling. I don't anticipate any intruders, but the magic is still new and stabilizing."

She turned and vanished into thin air.

"Well that's new." Ethan took a deep breath and let it out. "I guess it's damage control time. I'll see you guys there."

DOWNTOWN WAS LITTERED with plant parts and dried blood splatter. There was a crew still working on clearing it all up, but it was slow going. Tim was one of them, and was boarding up broken windows and fixing what he could.

Feya pulled herself from one of her trees and surveyed

the damage with a frown. She closed her eyes, rooted her bare toes into the ground, and sent out a call.

The air was silent and still for only a breath before an explosion of sound burst from the forest. Mice, rats, rabbits, and birds of all sizes chewed through the vines. A herd of deer came forward to help their small neighbors haul the debris into the woods to enrich the soil. Those humans who were out and about stood gaping. This was obviously not normal behavior for animals, but when a goddess calls, you respond.

Ground water rose up, flowing just over the surface, and washed away the bloodstains.

Vultures and crows descended from above. Coyotes yipped from nearby cornfields then trotted together down the main road. Insects scuttled from the grass and flies swarmed. The carrion creatures gathered all around and took care of any unclaimed remains.

A few crows dropped shiny objects such as coins and stolen car keys at Feya's feet.

"Why, thank you friends." She knelt and stroked their feathers.

People who had watched from close by warily approached now that the area was picked clean. She could hear them whispering about what they witnessed, and she chose to let them speculate on their own.

Ethan jogged from an alley brightly lit by the sun and offered her a hand to help her to her feet. She set her slender fingers in his rough palm and stood.

One of the crows hopped into the air then settled on Ethan's right shoulder. He smiled, and gave its neck a good scratch. The bird clicked its beak and settled in.

"My people!" Feya's voice rose above the chattering animals and conversation. "I have reclaimed my land. Some of you have proven to be true friends." Her gaze caught Tabby's, then roved over to Beverly. "From now until my end, this will be my home, and I shall rule all who remain."

Distressed voices rose in response, but none were directed specifically at her.

She raised her hands, recalling their attention. "I wasn't finished. I have decided to let those of you who wish to leave to do so. Immediately. Pack whatever belongings will fit in your vehicle and meet me at the edge of my territory at sundown. My wolves will escort you through the barrier." She swept a hand out to indicate Brian and his men. "But there is a catch."

Feya cast her gaze around once more, assessing her audience. Faces gazed towards her, some open and waiting, others stony or full of fear.

"If you choose to leave this place, you will never be allowed to return. In fact, as the town leaves your sight, you will forget Oak Grove. You'll simply have the urge to start over someplace new. You'll have a vague recollection of your former, but no desire to find this place again. As far as the outside world is concerned, Oak Grove is merely a legend."

A woman at the back of the crowd raised her hand.

Feya nodded to her.

"And what if we choose to stay? How will we live? The electricity is gone and most of us have jobs outside of town."

"I will not let my people fall to ruin. Those of you who farm should continue to do so. Those of you who have jobs outside of town will be able to leave and return. Your memory of home will be a bit hazy outside the barrier, but your instincts will lead you back. While we will continue to live outside the electrical grid, I can promise you clean water, good soil, and healthy livestock. Your families will continue to grow and prosper for as long as you remain loyal to me."

The woman who had asked the question nodded.

"You will also still be able to purchase goods and such. A post office will be built right outside of town, and your mail will continue to be delivered to you through post office boxes. Those of you that run businesses, I'll allow you to continue selling, but I would request that you begin focusing on local artisans and food sources."

While Feya continued delivering her rules and exceptions, Jenny began taking notes, earning her a position as the town secretary—or court scribe, as Feya later pronounced.

"Look around you," Feya commanded. "These are your people. Your neighbors. You will learn how to lean on one another. You will be there to help in times of crisis. If there's any trouble, bring your issues to the werewolves. They are here to keep this town safe."

"Does that make me the sheriff?" Brian called out, throwing an arm around his closest pack member.

"I suppose it does, if that's what you wish to be called. You are the guardians of this place," said Feya.

"Awesome!"

A smattering of laughter rang from the crowd, and they slowly broke apart. Those who chose to leave hurried to their homes and began packing as many belongings as they could, thankful that outside of Feya's little kingdom they would have access to their bank accounts and no conscious memory of the horrors they'd witnessed.

"Well then, my lady." Ethan lifted Feya's chin with the knuckle of his first finger. "How should we spend the remainder of our day?"

"Oh, I think we should celebrate." Her arms slid

around his neck, and her fingers toyed with the hair at his nape.

"What are you proposing?"

Instead of answering, she tipped up and met his mouth with her own.

As THE SUN lowered in the sky, Tabby watched as a line of vehicles passed her shop.

She was one of Feya's newly-minted council members and had spent the day making arrangements, charting, and going over plans to help her neighbors build up their gardens. She decided classes were in order, so she set about making lists of things she'd need to form a curriculum.

The rumble of engines and tires on the road had stirred her from her work. She'd come to the front of her shop and leaned against the railing. She wanted to be surprised by the number of families leaving—people she'd known her whole life—but deep down, she knew a majority of the citizens of Oak Grove would leave and forget.

The last taillight passed, and she returned to her work.

20

A group of high school kids roamed the town, hauling water and helping people gather supplies. Others came together with various tools and were working on clearing the side roads.

The vines themselves began sprouting more of the football sized flower buds. Tabitha poked gently at one, and found it to be firm to the touch. They were faintly scented, the sweetness attracting bees like starving men to a feast. The ants also paid special attention to them.

"Well hello there," Tabby said to a particularly small bee resting on a bud in front of her. The bee ignored her and went about its business.

Once upon a time, she'd had ambitions to become a beekeeper. She hadn't had the time for it, but the empty hives remained in a shed behind her shop, collecting years-worth of dust. She hadn't a clue how to lure the bees to her hives beyond finding a queen.

In the meantime, she headed to her shed, severing vines to get to the door, unlocked it, and sneezed as she stepped inside. Dust indeed. And buzzing. Lots of buzzing.

Using the little flashlight she'd shoved into her pocket earlier, she shone a beam at the corner of the room. Hundreds of bees crawled up the wall, congregating in one corner.

"Well then." Her mutters were heard by no one as she approached the tarp covered bee boxes. Glancing over at the buzzing mass, just to be sure of her distance, she yanked the material back. There were a lot of boxes, more than she remembered. Apparently, she'd been quite ambitious.

She checked them over for any damage and was satisfied that they were in as good condition as when she'd bought them.

"I'll be back. Don't go anywhere." She squinted at the bees and shook a finger at them, before giggling to herself and heading to her shop to retrieve the hand truck she used to move inventory around.

Soon, she had a few hauled out into the yard.

"Whatcha doin' Ms. Richards?" A boy she vaguely recognized from school events called from the road way.

"Hopefully capitalizing on all the bees that have come to investigate the mutant vines." She tapped the side of a box with a hollow thunk.

"Need a hand?"

Tabby gave the boy one of her brightest smile. "That's the best offer I've had all day. Yes, I'd absolutely love a hand with these."

Together, they moved the boxes to the back yard and settled them on the most level space in the yard.

"Thanks—?" Tabby dropped off, still not remembering the kid's name.

"Matt. And any time Ms. R." He grinned in return, leaning against the last hive.

"What's all this?" Feya appeared seemingly from nowhere.

"Son of a fish nugget!" Tabby yelped, slapping a hand to her heart.

"What's a fish nugget?" the dryad asked.

"No idea. It just sorta popped out. I'm setting up bee hives. Now I just have to figure out how to get them out of my shed and into these boxes. I'm off to do some research."

"Oh, I can help with that." Feya headed into the shed, reemerging moments later with a handful of bees.

She brought them close for Tabby to see, then opened her hands, letting the bees crawl all around her fingers. "See the queen?"

"Whoa! How'd you do that?" Matt asked, leaning in for a closer look.

"Matt, this is Feya, our local dryad and part of the reason why things have all gone wacky." Tabby gave the boy a warning look, hoping he wouldn't say anything that would upset the creature.

"Oh! Okay. I'll do my best to stay on your good side." He winked and flashed a dimpled grin.

Feya smiled at him, then lightly stroked the queen with her index finger. "Let me get her to her new home."

Tabby lifted the lid of the box and watched as the dryad gently set the tiny insects atop the frames. Her fingers danced around the wood, and the bees darted forward to watch.

"What are you doing?" Matt asked, leaning in to watch the bees crawl around.

"Letting them know what's going on: That this is their new home, and they should spread the news."

Several bees took off, flitting on the breeze.

"They'll tell all their friends. Hopefully this is enough hives." Feya took the lid from Tabby and fit it into place.

"That is so cool! How'd you learn to talk to them?"

Feya shrugged. "Instinct. Intuition. Something like that. I've known the local hives for a very long time."

"So cool!" Matt said again.

The air began to vibrate, and a dark cloud rapidly approached.

"What the actual—" Tabby's jaw dropped as a swarm of hundreds of thousands of bees descended towards the hives, the sound of their wings deafening.

The trio watched as new homes were claimed, while others alighted in a nearby tree.

"It's hollow." Feya explained. "Still alive though. They should make a home of it for a time."

Tabby stood stock still as bees crawled all over her. She'd never been afraid of them, valuing them for their essential work connected with her own, but this was way more than she'd ever seen before.

Feya's eyebrows rose. "I think you may have lost possession of your shed."

Tabby groaned. "I've got so many tools in there. How can I get to them without disturbing the hives?"

"Easy," Feya said, "I'll get them for you."

Tabby eyed the group of bees inspecting her sleeve. "Well, thanks."

The dryad reached out and gently brushed the bees from her. "What are friends for?"

THE GIANT RASPBERRY vines were cut away from fields, houses, and businesses but still ran through abandoned buildings and patches of forest. The blooms sprang open about a week after the town emptied of all those who'd wished to leave, bathing the town in a fruity sweet breeze.

Tabby and Sara set up the shop for their first gardening class with chairs borrowed from the church and 3 ring binders from the general store bartered for with produce from the greenhouses. Making copies had been tedious at first until a neighbor offered up their generator so she could use her computer and printer.

No longer having to pay a mortgage on her business and personal property, Tabby threw a good chunk of her remaining money into a couple windmills and set ups for solar panels so she could just about go back to life as normal. Another chunk of money went into her savings while the rest was invested. Everything in town ran on a barter system now, so money was only needed for purchases outside of town. Feya had liked Tabby's plan so much, she'd brought it up at the next town meeting, suggesting that others implement it for themselves.

The request for generators, however, she turned down. She'd claimed she couldn't guarantee the prosperity of the land with all that gas about, but she allowed them to use up what they already had.

What Tabby wouldn't give for a hot shower. Her baths now consisted of a bucket of water that she sometimes heated up over a fire. Usually, she just dealt with the cold. She'd probably be okay with it for the summer, but she dreaded sponge baths in February if she didn't get her energy sources up and running before then.

Tim moved in with Tabby, just as they'd planned while Lucas and Jenny moved into Tim's old house, just down the road. Jenny flat out refused to step foot in her childhood home again, so Lucas and Tabby had retrieved the rest of her things and settled them in their new home.

It felt odd, not having her son at home anymore. Yes,

he was her neighbor, but he was also her child and would always be her child. He might have turned 18 with a good head on his shoulders, but that wouldn't stop her from worrying.

Tim broke open a pack of ballpoint pens and slid two into each binder which already held graph paper and a few sample layouts for gardens.

A knock called her attention to the front door, and Feya let herself in. The dryad had continued wearing her renaissance inspired wardrobe. It suited her. She looked every inch the queen goddess with the sweeping fabric and her wild looks.

"I like that plumb color on you." Tabby wove her way through the chairs to give her friend a hug. Despite all that had happened, they were still friends. Tabby addressed her more formally in public, but in private, she'd always see her ruler as the young girl who'd shown up at her door.

"Thanks!" Feya wrapped her arms around Tabby, squeezing her back. "Is there anything I can do to help?"

Tabby cocked an eyebrow. "Don't you have some queenly duty to perform?"

Feya shrugged. "That's why I have minions—I mean werewolves."

Throwing her head back, Tabby laughed. "Your sense of humor is growing."

From across the room, Sara snorted.

"I'm learning the rules of jesting." Feya nodded, flipping through one of the binders.

"Don't you make the rules?"

Feya tapped her lips with her index finger. "That's true. I do. I say I'm hilarious, and everyone must laugh at all my jokes."

Tabby snorted. "Good luck with that edict. Anyway, if you really want to help, would you mind looking at my map? I'm trying to plot out what crops would grow best where. I don't know how people will feel about switching produce, but I really do want us to thrive as a community, and I'd like to be able to make the most helpful suggestions."

"That's a wonderful idea." Feya followed her friend behind the counter where a map of the town lay spread out on the back work table. Feya grabbed a pen and began making notes, calculating what she knew of the soil health in certain areas and how the weather affected the landscape directly on the map.

Ethan arrived next, breathing hard as if he'd been running. "Feya, the wolves are looking for you."

"Oh for fuck's sake, what is it now?" Feya continued muttering as she headed towards her mate. She paused at the door and turned. "I'll be back to work on that some more later. I apparently have 'queenly tasks' to take care of after all."

Tabby suppressed more laughter at Feya's cursing. The dryad had picked up swearing with gusto and used it whenever just because she could.

SEVERAL MONTHS LATER, Lucas sat his mother down at The Sip Down and announced that Jenny was pregnant.

The news had taken Tabby by surprise. Luke had insisted they'd been careful, and she could tell he was scared.

"Everything's going to be just fine." Tabby gathered her wits, then took Luke's hands in her own. "Why don't you two come over for dinner, and we'll talk some more and start making plans. What is it you're most worried about?"

He studied the coffee in his mug. "We're just kids. We're not ready."

"That's probably true, but no one is ever ready. Babies don't come with owner's manuals, and every child is different." She smiled at him. "I lucked out when I got you."

"Thanks Mom, but I don't know how that's supposed to make me feel better." He dropped his forehead to the table.

Patting his head, she said, "It's not. This is something I can't decide for you. The choices you've made have led to this. That's life. How's Jenny feel about it?"

"Well, she's ecstatic. She's making all sorts of plans, talking about things that will have to change around the house."

"So you're overwhelmed and are feeling like you're being replaced."

"How do you do that?" Lucas sat up and crossed his arms over his chest, glaring across the table at his mother.

"Do what?" She sipped her tea with a dainty raise of her pinky.

"Pinpoint exactly what's going on in my head."

"Oh, sweetheart." She reached across and patted his cheek. "I raised you, and I pay attention."

He snorted at that.

"We'll figure this out. If the problem is the house, we'll help you get it straightened out. If you need support, we're here for you. And I hope it's okay, but I'm excited too."

"You just want to hold a baby. I hate to break it to you, but it's like the size of a lima bean right now. You're gonna have to wait."

"Oh, I'll wait, but that's not going to stop me from spoiling them rotten."

"Mo-om!" he groaned.

THE RASPBERRIES HARVESTED from the mutant vines tasted unlike anything anyone in the little kingdom had ever eaten before. Beverly already had a cellar full of newly bottled mead she'd made with the berries and honey from Tabby's hives.

The town might grow sick of eating the new fruit eventually, but they'd begun profiting off of canned goods, sweets, and so much more they'd brought beyond the barrier. Their branding was all based on the Oak Grove dryad legend, which pleased Feya greatly.

Inside the barrier, Feya's people were thriving. Squabbles were quickly ended when the werewolves got involved. No one particularly wanted to mess with them.

The banshee had wailed only once so far when an elderly citizen passed peacefully in his sleep. The cry had sent a chill through the town. People locked their doors as the creature, formerly Mary, glided through town and came to rest under the old man's window howling until Feya came forward and dismissed her. The body was still warm as she carried it from the house and through town to the church. Family and friends gathered and prepared the body. He was to be buried at the edge of the original grove, at the base of a young sapling, which would mark his resting place for years to come.

Feya left them to it. She would preside over the graveside funeral when they were ready.

When it was time, she carried the wrapped body and set it gently on the ground atop its final resting place, several yards from where Rachelle was laid to rest. Everyone said their goodbyes, then the sapling reached its roots from the soil and welcomed the body into its new home. The next day, a patch of lady slippers, covered the grave.

Seasons turned and people passed while others were born. Sara and Brian became good friends before falling in love and moving in together.

Lucas and Jenny named their brand new baby Rachelle after the much-loved minister. Despite mistakes made and nights on end without sleep, Luke immediately fell in love with his tiny baby girl. Tabby got her hands on her grandbaby whenever she could and of course spoiled her rotten.

Feya gave the baby a blessing, though she wouldn't – or perhaps couldn't – tell anyone what it was, having been inspired by the sleeping beauty story. It became a tradition that Feya would bless every newborn within her kingdom a week after the birth.

Slowly, the barrier's magic did its job of erasing Oak Grove. While it appeared on maps printed before the event, cartographers simply forgot to include it on new ones. Though now considered fictional, Oak Grove was able to sustain itself on the production and sales of the giant raspberries. The myth simply made those products more alluring to the rest of the world, especially since no one could figure out where they actually came from or how they had found their way into stores.

Feya ruled over all who remained through magic and secret. Some followed her out of fear, others of loyalty, and with a very few, love.

EPILOGUE

"I swear, this is the place the wine comes from."

A redheaded woman in her early 20's climbed out of the passenger side of the red Ford Focus her friend was driving. She stomped down into the ditch, then up to the edge of the woods on the other side. She pulled a fallen branch away from a sign that had seen better days. The wood was chipped, and the paint was so faded and damaged she almost couldn't read the words "Oak Grove population—" The number of residents was gouged away with what looked like a massive stroke of claws.

"See?" She turned to her friend, hands on hips, triumphant.

"Yeah, whatever. Get your ass back in the car, Megan." The brunette leaned out her window and waved her friend back.

Megan trudged back and slammed the door, buckling herself back in. "Keep driving, Izzy."

"Babe, this is barely a logging road. Nobody is going to come pull us out if we get stuck." Despite her words, Izzy shifted her car into drive.

10 minutes went by, and the two young women weren't getting anywhere. There were no houses, businesses, or even a road sign. Just endless trees.

Megan suddenly bolted straight and pointed. "Look, Izz, there's someone walking up the road! Maybe they can give us directions."

Izzy leaned forward, squinting. "Maybe. If not, we're turning around."

"You're the boss," said Megan, still sitting forward in her seat.

As they drew closer to the figure, they found it was a woman, dressed in a fancy forest green dress. She smiled and approached the car as it slowed to a stop.

ANYONE CAN FIND Oak Grove on an old map. But those who go looking for it always find themselves hopelessly lost on a neglected road in the middle of nowhere until they decide to turn back.

Some say a strange woman in a long, dark dress appears on the road before them. If you stop and speak with her, she'll give you directions to anywhere but Oak Grove.

DEAR READER,

Thank you for picking up my book! Malediction was so different from Beasts Among Us. The tone, the style... the sex!

I hope you enjoyed diving into this new world with me. I have every intention for this book to be a stand alone, but the world has barely been explored, so there's always a chance I'll get sucked back into Feya's little pocket kingdom.

As with many of my books, this one began as a NaNoWriMo project. Did I win the year I wrote it? No. Did I mean for there to be any romance whatsoever? Also no. Malediction was meant to be purely a fantasy horror. It does have both those elements, but I couldn't get Feya and Ethan to keep their paws off each other!

Another surprise was the relationship between Tabby and Luke. Luke was going to be sort of a background character, but when this mother/son duo started their verbal sparring and showing me how much they loved each other, I happily embraced it.

steps on stool Loved it or hated it, please review it! It

really helps authors gain visibility. And while I know it's considered a no-no for authors to read reviews on their books, sometimes I can't help myself. There are aways gonna be people you can't please, but sometimes there's a gem with beautiful well thought out criticism. (One ARC reviewer from one of my other books was so good, I asked her to join my beta team for the rest of that series!) There will always be flaws. Typos, especially, are dirty little ninjas that will sneak by countless rounds of edits on my end, beta readers, and even professional editors. A good review, at any star rating, is worth everything.

steps off stool ahem. Anyhow. I hope you enjoyed Feya's story! So what do *you* think? Is she a villain or victim?

Love always,
   Jen

P.s. Come follow me at all the places with my link tree!

ACKNOWLEDGMENTS

First off, I'd like to thank my husband. He lives with my bookishness with so much grace. Both with my collecting and production of books. He's the level head to my chaos and I can't imagine doing life without him.

Next is my beta readers for this project: Tracie and Kat. I told them to give it to me straight. I'd rather hear the bad news while editing than after I hit publish. And boy did they! They've both pushed me to be a better writer and that's priceless. And to the rest of the Nomadic Guild of Scripturients, you guys are awesome and I miss meet-ups. Hopefully life will put us all on similar schedules again soon!

To my editor, Lea: Thank you for helping Malediction shine! I'm so grateful we happened upon each other. You're a beautiful soul and friend.

To my street team: Despite the stop/go thing I had going on with this book (organization, what?) you all are aways there to support me.

To my reader group, The Zamboni Pack's Lair on FB: I may not be good at giving updates/consistency, yet you're still there, and that means the world to me.

Lastly, to everyone who reads my books. Thank you for taking a chance on me. If you're new here, welcome. If you've been following all along, I love you!

About the Author

Jennifer Zamboni is an urban fantasy author from central Maine. She lives with her husband, two tiny tornados (daughters), and her menagerie of pets. When she's not reading or writing she likes to knit and embroider.

Check out https://linktr.ee/Jenniferzamboni to keep up to date!

ALSO BY JENNIFER ZAMBONI

Beasts Among Us

Beauty is the Beast

Pack of Freaks

Worlds War

Short Stories

Werewolves, Water, & War: A Beasts Among Us short story